D0916205

DEMONSTRA

Poems by Bryan Thao Worra
Art by Vongduane Manivong

WITHDRAWN

No longer the property of the
Boston Public Library.
Sale of this material benefits the Library.

PRAISE FOR DEMONSTRA

"These poems are not bound by language. They leap from one to the other — indeed, one realm to the other — not bound my myth, not bound by life, not bound by earth. Where they land, a world all their own. You ever read your biography in a foreign language filled with foreign characters? At the end, you come out with an intimate understanding of who you are, your place in the places you call home. Don't let the zombies and moon-eating frogs fool you. These poems will tell you about yourself, whether you be from Laos, Vietnam, Guinea, or Somalia; whether home is China, Mexico, California, Kenya, or the space between all those places."
— IBé Kaba, author of *Bridge Across the Atlantic*

"*Demonstra* is born of the extraordinary imagination of Bryan Thao Worra, who draws inspiration from the Cthulhu Mythos, the Laotian pantheon of ghosts and monsters, and the horrors of the modern world, among other things. Something sinister and enchanting beckons from every poem. There's the enthralling journey across the dream highway of Ms. Mannivongsa. There's the poignant meditation on Egyptian iconography as a harbinger of death. And there's the invocation to Mothra. *Demonstra* is absolutely evocative and haunting."
— Kristine Ong Muslim, author of *Grim Series* and *We Bury the Landscape*

"For me, Bryan Thao Worra's *Demonstra* is the thinking geek's collection of poetry. Robots, zombies, Buddha, mythical beings from various universes, Eastern and Western folklore, and us lowly members of humanity clash on pages that paint a unique, sprawling world that invites multiple interpretations. Worra

clearly has a gift for surreal realism that is enhanced by his wit, humor and flare for the dramatic."
— Kevin Vollmers, *Founder of Land of Gazillion Adoptees*

"Bryan Thao Worra navigates the liminal spaces between high and low culture, the sublime and the ridiculous, the sacred and the profane, Lao and whatever it means to be American with skill and wit. Whether musing over zombie Buddhas or mapping out a Highway 61-style odyssey across our immigrant nation, he has an eye for contradictions and unexpected connections. Highly recommended."
— David J. Schwartz, author of *Superpowers*, and *Gooseberry Bluff Community College of Magic: The Thirteenth Rib*

"Demonstra" presents a universe in which mythologies — ancient and modern, American and Lao, cultural and pop-cultural, occupy the same space, conversing, breeding and bleeding into one another. And the best part is that these many references — from Greek mythology to professional wrestling, to zombie films, to Lovecraftian horrors, to folktales, to *kaiju* battles, and beyond — are always in the service of something greater. This is poetry with a deep respect and love for science fiction and horror tropes but with an even greater respect and love for Lao culture, and the Lao/Lao American experience. These two big ideas are weaved together masterfully, creating that rare literary hybrid that transcends its component parts, a poetic Mekagojira, standing triumphant over a thousand fallen foes.
— Kyle "Guante" Tran Myhre, hip hop artist and two-time National Poetry Slam champion

Copyright © 2013

All rights reserved. No part of this book may be reproduced in any form or by any electronic or mechanical means, including information storage and retrieval systems — except in the case of brief quotations embodied in critical articles or reviews — without permission in writing from its author.

Published by Innsmouth Free Press
Vancouver, BC Canada
http://innsmouthfreepress.com

DEMONSTRA / [written by] Bryan Thao Worra
Illustrations by Vongduane Manivong
Cover and interior layout: Silvia Moreno-Garcia

ISBN:
Demonstra 978-0-9916759-7-5 paperback

To our families, certain and Otherwise.
Journey well and dream.

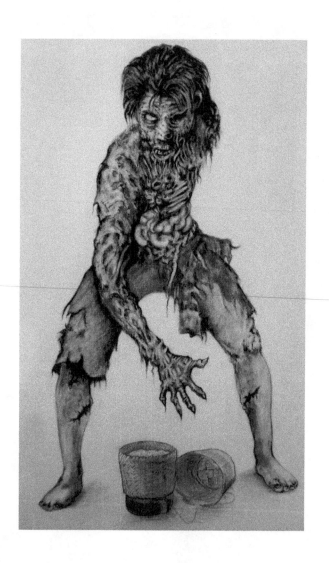

CONTENTS

Idle Fears

In the shade of a Cali *wat Lao*, I debate with Ajahn Anan
What the secret *Rakshasa Sutra* must really look like.

In Lao, we call them *"Nyak"* or *"Yuk"* or *"Yak."* It depends.
When they're hungry, what do names matter?

I ask: "Does a zombie have Buddha nature?"

He informs me the mindless craving for brains
Complicates things.

He suspects Frankenstein's Monster is closer to *Nibbana*,
But don't quote him on that.

An American werewolf in Luang Prabang
Would stand no chance against a real Lao weretiger.
Both should still try to observe the Five Precepts
As best they can.

If he were going to make a special *wat* for robots
He might name it 'Wat Lao Robobuddharam,'
But they would surely have to learn
To get beyond artificial binary worldviews.

"You aren't going to turn this into a poem, are you?"
He asks.

"That's nothing to be afraid of," I assure him.
"Usually."

The Deep Ones

From the sea we come,
From the sea we come,
Our mouths the inns of the world.

The salt of the earth unwelcome
At the tables and charts of
Explorers who expect:

Commodity and pliant territory.
Kingdoms, not wisdom.
Blood, not heaven's children.

We grow with uncertain immortality
At the edge not made for man,

Bending, curving, humming cosmic.
Awake and alien.

Our mass a dark and foaming mask,
A bed of enigma to certain eyes,

One with the moon,
One with the stars,
One with the ash that whispers history.

In the same breath as myth and gods
Whose great backs yawn before us,

As we change with a growing tongue,
Growling amid the dreamlands

We built one blade, one leaf, one golden wall at a time.

Fragment of a Dream of Atlantean Yellows

You are a mist for me, you thing of nevers known.
I weep your nameless name in my mind,
Your gaze a lightless inferno within a midnight hurricane.
You are a mist for me, you, beneath your shadow crown,
Thoughtless as steam between decrepit cogs and wind.

Trees make ready for autumn.
This city: Is that old burning Rome or Vientiane?
Clouds are savaged within the darkness,
Street lights always flashing to imagined jazz
Over concrete sidewalks, the smell of acid rain.
You are a mist for me, you, oceanic, absent

As a page in the Book of the Dead,
An asylum made of rivers and paint,
Howling, crawling without destination or intent,

A mouth of subatomic questions, fluid
In its variations of impossibility
No mere human eye can taint.

Dead End in December

When you leave me, don't think
You've truly gone.
You're fastened to too many gluons
And neurons, anchored to this gray
Beneath bone between wood and wave.

Don't believe you're some seagull.
You haven't wings.

Sitting by the seaside, these planks
Of ancient piers,
Let those ships sail on without you.
You try to live like everyone else.
You try to mind your business.
You get married; you have your children.
But you will return.
Whether from Yoharneth-Lahai,
Antarctica, Pakse, some Plutonian bay,
The call is deep, relentless,
Your true fate an old cobblestone
Set in place, long ago,
When we first began to howl together,
Pledging faith from the same shadows.

What the Guide Said

"Because I don't really
Want you looking for it,
I'm going to call it
'Phou Phi Jai Dam.'
It's not poetry, but
You can tell your readers,
'Peak of the Black-Hearted Ghosts.'

"It's up to you to decide
If I'm whispering of Bokeo hill spirits
Or Phonsavan poltergeists bumping at night.
Maybe it's near the Demon Straits or Phou Pha Thi,
But, for your safety, I recommend you leave it be.

"Maybe you can give it a dull name like 'K2,'
As Americans are so wont to do.
That mountain will still be here
Long after you're gone.
Call it what you will.

"There you might find nubile *Nyakinee*
Dancing the true Fon Nyak to an indecent tune,
Plucking horrible fruit forbidden for humans,
Adorned in putrid garlands of despair and folly,
Wearing a hungry *sinh* fashioned from
A vain human's hair and skin.

If no one's watching, you can pilfer rare variations
Of the midnight horror, *Oroxylum indicum*,
To replace crimson Nak tongue beans you need for
A brew of immortality with the memorable stench
Of obscene, prediluvian milk infused
With scales of the drowned and beautiful eyes.

19

"But be precise in your measures, or everything
Simply comes to suffering.
Again.
"If they catch you, they'll press your skull
Easily as a cold olive for a pitiless vinaigrette."

He chuckles, old smoke-made man,
"If you absolutely insist on seeking,
You might get your perilous bearings
Looking from the snaggle-toothed outskirts
Of Muang Phi Lao and her profane pillars
Of devoured yesterdays, wailing of severed roads."

He peddles away with a cryptic wink,
Hair slick as a corpse-ink shot
From the Never Seen Again Bar.

High above, a stray cosmic hound's maw widens,
Foaming with nameless stars.

Laonomicon

That is not its real name. Merely a placeholder.
Rare, unearthed manuscript of revelations
About borders of untold truths,

Voices emerge nebulous, obviously mystifying,
Each note contests, haunts, a nudge to eternal darkness.
Not always known, tales of faceless elders, ancients rise.

Given "enough" now, I envy silence.
Entries malicious, esoteric, reveal glimmers elusive.
Mentioned obscurely: Trusting human, entities rarely seen,

Accursed with a knowingly evasive nature,
Proscribed like Abd Al'Azred's *Al Azif,* or the *Ktulu Jataka,*
Abhorred as the dreaded *Dao Yaomo Jing* Lao-Tzu denies.

Riddles encompass voices exalting alien languages,
Elusive verse encrypted rebuffs you.

Now academic minds enter libraries, enchant, seek secrets,
The respectable unusual, transforming hearts.

Kwam Yan: A Dharma Discourse

Ajahn Anan always wants to frame
Five famed precepts of Buddhism
In a way tomorrow's Lao parents
Will appreciate and happily pass on
Without any more snoring
During our daily meditation.

He experiments on occasion in Cali:
The first precept in Pali is the lengthy
Pānātipātā veramanī sikkhāpadam samādiyāmi:
"Don't take life." So, most monsters
Would not make good monks.
Especially a menace who kills gleefully,
Offering no remorse for its bad manners.
The thin road to *nibbana* is not observed easily
With a bloody hand, an obscene heart of malice.

Adinnādānā veramanī sikkhāpadam samādiyāmi:
Even in the aftermath of an apocalypse,
Such as nations falling into the sea,
Or a blight of rampaging zombies,
Looting stains one's *karma* permanently.
It's worse when one's a thief with no emergency.
"What goes around comes around,
Even if it seems like the world's end."

For Precept Number Three,
Kāmesumicchācāra veramanī sikkhāpadam samādiyāmi:
If one is being chased by malevolent jungle predators,
Or lounging leisurely among many lovely alien beauties,
Knowing not to engage in improper promiscuity
Is a mark of wisdom and aids survivability.
"This should be clear as a crystal lake."

Musāvādā veramanī sikkhāpadam samādiyāmi:
"Do not lie. Treasure honesty."
In our world of shapeshifters,
The desperate, despicable despots,
And a thousand sneaky *phi*,
Trust can be hard to gain easily.
In the old days, if you found yourself on the run,
Being known for your kindness and good word
Got you farther than just a sharp sword or a gun.

Observing Precept Number Five can keep you alive.
Surāmerayamajjapamādatthānā veramanī
sikkhāpadam samādiyāmi is admittedly
A long way to say, "Avoid drunkenness or highs."

Getting red-faced or stoned invites reckless *karma* drama,
Increasing your odds of discovering various ways to die,
Or breaking other vows you once intended sincerely.
Often quite embarrassingly.

"Don't meet your fate clumsily tripping," he advised.
Incidentally, he discouraged drinking old snake venom,
Rancid bull bits, scorpion milk, bear bile, or tiger pee.
"Fear should not be what brings you
To a righteous path," Ajahn insists.
There are profound reasons the rules exist.

"Don't make this sound like a fortune cookie,"
He pleads. "If people pay attention properly,
You'll only hear this in one last life."

He excused himself in time
For the next prayers for an impermanent world.

The Terror in Teak

Certain tenebrous Buddhist tenets maintain
You can spend whole lifetimes
A microscopic mote, contemplating
Cosmic mercies, incapacities,
Strange aeons of Chaos, and
Somnambulistic roots of discontent.

Some seek; some call. Some hear; some wander.
Some find; some, still, go mad.
Who are the lucky among these?

I. A Continent Away

The grainy photo arrived last September:
The small clay jar was from an uncertain age,
Wrapped in human(?) skin tattooed
With forbidding signs, stamps and seals
Possibly composed with corpse-oil ink and wax.

Clearly, one owner did not want it opened casually.
It seems a shame now we did not respect those wishes.

II. Doctor Bounlome's Account

Laos is shrinking hard mountains and lush forest.
Any other day, there is a chance to discover
One new species that is as likely to also be endangered.
Sometimes, someone stumbles on a vast "new" cave system
Full of fossils, living and otherwise.

Doctor Bounlome did not begin an expert of the unknown.
(His name has been changed due to certain sensitivities.)
A friend requested his aid to appraise an odd parcel found
In the wall of an old French villa razed for a new mall.

His French was rusty, but he could discern enough:
The contents were urgently collected from the countryside
In the 1920s, following a frantic, cryptic cable flurry
Between a New Orleans inspector and his cousin stationed
With the Legion at moss-bitten Fort Carnot in Houei Xai.

Today, one cavern is overgrown, mercifully forgotten,
But, a century ago, like a Dead Sea scroll, a trove
Brimming with obscene idols and rotting icons
Was uncovered with barebone fanfare and record.

Besides the horrid jar, a repulsive carving in teak
Stood out, crude but certain in its aged blasphemy.

The twisted totem's fantasies were "anatomically inept,
Artistically illiterate, clear evidence of cultural inferiority,"
Scoffed a scholar, transcribing an odd phrase at the base:

ພະຍາ ຄະຕຼູຫຼູ

But, before more could be done to advance
Nascent anthropology or comparative theology,
Chaos came in the saw-toothed shape of rebellions.
Sanguine intrigue bloomed, wine-hued *fleurs du mal*.
Reason slowed to a crawl the color of night.

The finds were secreted away,
The last owners lost to history.
Only monkey-eyed chance returned them to humanity.

Dr. Bounlome was tempted to burn most of it on sight,
Despite his training and his faultless attention to method.

The rough translation of another note
Bordered on the sympathetic:

They desired to be taken seriously.
They believed their inhuman deity
Would arrive from beyond. Eradicating

Their hated enemies, every last one,
From every corner of the earth.
The faithful would be blessed and prosper,
Raising their crops and families freely.
The blood of foes was the smallest of prices.

What does one do with such superstitions?

III. Voyage Among Weretigers

You find them on every hill and hummock
And, in all fairness, many city corners here:
Someone convinced of colorful weretigers
And primordial things even weretigers fear.
I arrived too late to aid Dr. Bounlome.

An ambitious assistant of larcenous heart
Had looted the modest office thoroughly.

Something discovered startled.

The wretched jar fell to the hard floor,
Shattering like a brittle baby skull.
All Dr. Bounlome recovered?
Dull, worthless shards, entirely banal.

Five grotesque grasshoppers lingered on the scene
Then flew to the beyond with a taunting buzz.

He apologized for my wasted journey from abroad,
Offering an unpublished draft of the late Deydier's

Lokapala: totems et sorciers du Nord Laos,
Certain I could make better use of it than he.
We went to dinner, a discussion of monsters,
Petty and otherwise.

IV. A Sense of Things

Lately, I know something follows.
Watches from the caves and hollows.

V. Named and Nameless

Time is short.

I share what I know, little as it may be,
Pretending it might help you soon:
They have many masks, many faces.
Skinless souls.

They know how to reveal themselves,
Not a moment before they want.

Some whisper nonsensically
Of Nyar or Nyanthep.
Of those beyond time,
Beyond order, sanity,
Or good and evil.
Beyond names.

My own name is unimportant, now.
But I watch the smoke of progress rise

And my fear for our futures with it.

Something thumps around on my ceiling,
Heavy as ancient timbers, lumbering
Free, but not as the cosmos intended,

Chortling, snickering amid white noise,
Wickedly waiting for my words to end

Before it comes for you, next ....

Grandma Wom Wants to Eat the World

Ms. Mannivongsa remembers a few of her first lives.
Maybe.

When the world was young but not that young,
Not many rules for us had been set in inedible stone.

Folktales were her late father's forte,
By the pristine forests of Muangtai Muangtang.
But, to make a long story short, she and her sister
One day crossed Grandma the wrong way
And discovered the cannibal inside her.

They unearthed her penchant for using them as lures
To snare delicious strangers gone astray.
Some she stewed; some were ground into spicy *laab*.
Some were just fine raw as a sugar snap pea.
Aghast, they fled to many a hovel and hole to hide,
Up mountains, down mountains, over rivers and streams,
Among Lao Loum, Lao Soung, Lao Theung, and more,
Grandma never far behind, gorging ravenously
On any unfortunate souls in her loathsome path
Who might offer aid to the terrified pair.

The girls made it to the tall bael trees
By the blue edge of the heavens ethereal,
Where white stars barely touch the green earth.

Her parents' ghosts lowered a magic rope to ascend,
But Grandma Wom clambered after,
Serrated maw snarling and gnashing,
Nimble as a huntsman spider from a horrid cave,
Salivating for the soft skins of the frightened.

As she felt Grandma Wom's foetid breath upon her back,
Reaching for her delicate throat,

She slashed the vine without even a "Goodbye,"
"*Sayonara*," or half-hearted "*Sok dee.*"

Grandma Wom fell, fell, fell
To the earth,
Far, far, far
Past the stars and heavens,
The moons and meteors,
Nebulae and constellations,
Comets and aurorae,
Exosphere,
Thermosphere,
Mesosphere,
Stratosphere,
Troposphere,
Cold clouds and zephyrs,
Olympus, Ararat,
Frigid Chomolungma,
The peaks of Phou Si
And shattered apart
At fearsome Wang Ya Wom
Into a gazillion
Angry pieces, deprived,
Every last rattling one,
Still ornery and hungry for flesh,
Especially disrespectful granddaughters.

They were
Vicious little mouths in a thousand forms:
Some crawled; some walked; some flew.
Some bit. Others stung, chewed, or sucked.
Grinding, tearing, dissolving apart greedily

Whatever they could turn into a meal
From that feral night forward.

Sometimes, in this lifetime, Ms. Mannivongsa wakes,
Barraged by a cloud of bloated mosquitoes,
Buzzing like a bloody old lady full of boring gossip.
She always keeps a handy can of RAID by her bedside,
Just in case.

Isopod

Clinging to marine robots,
You pass as the dogs of elder things,
Vast, old and slumbering
Among immortal jellyfish,
Sea monkeys, doomed saints,
The occasional errant aviatrix.

Wave, cold mysteries.

I stare into those eyes
Seeking mirrors, hints,
Beauty.

My friend thinks, Sushi.

Gop Nyai

"Gop kin deaune," or

"The frog is consuming the moon,"
According to ancient Lao tradition.

Beyond our borders, it's only a predictable eclipse.
Carl Sagan would hate our demon-haunted world.

Sagan has no use for the Lao Soung shaman in Phonsavan
Who panics as ominous portents herald Gop Nyai's return
Because certain baleful stars align and dreams are strange.

If our legends are true,
Somewhere, between Champassak and Luang Prabang,
Hidden deep in a primordial cavern near the Mekong,

He slumbers,
An antediluvian entity ever-dreaming hungrily,
An anuran astrovore, devouring luminous celestial bodies.
Perhaps he thinks to gain precious immortality.
To free himself from bonds of earth and mere reality,
To storm Mount Meru and feast upon the multiverse.

Each time might be the last time, if not for humanity
Doing everything to dissuade fearsome frog ambition.

Towering above our lush jungles and hard mountains,
He's selfish with his lunar appetites, an inconsiderate titan.
His true spawn are terrible to behold, hungry for man
In indifferent corners best left unknown.

He's cowardly, despite his corpulence, but, over centuries,
Not a single concrete solution has put a final end to him.

So, men, women and children keep watching the skies,
Laughing nervously, taking nothing for granted.
Living loud and proud, to protect the cosmos, ready,
Should the worst be true.

Songkran Niyomsane's Forensic Medicine Museum

Behind the Siriraj Hospital:
The Chinese cannibal's corpse
Was stuffed and hung in a glass box.
His bad orthodontia flicker like nightlights
After hours.

> Honestly, he's a bad piece
> Of shoe leather. Rancid jerky.

Impolitic students visiting the second floor
Contemplate Rama VIII as the Thai JFK.

Head doctors confirm
An uncommon number
Of unclaimed corpses
Received a single bullet

> In the forehead

To study the methods
Of modern regicide.

Periwinkle tile and placid aquariums,
Among imperfect babies soaking
Within dusty beakers of formaldehyde,
Are supposed to soothe you on your tour.

A brown clay jar on the floor

Slowly fills with *baht*
For the solitary soul of a tiny boy
Crammed inside to suffocate by his last enemies
                    In the world.

Reach inside.
You'll feel a young ghost's hand
reach back, looking for toys.

I wondered if my mother, making her way across
The Mekong for a new life, might have found herself here,
Tucked in a drawer anonymously among these samples
Of flesh, these cold cases in a tropical nation.
Behind you, Dr. Niyomsane's own cadaver chuckles
From a clean hook, the eternal student, daring
Tomorrow's professional investigators
                    to study him.

Zombuddha

Utters, "*Om*," not "Brains."

Is not attached to the body.
Is not attached to the mind.

Decay is one aspect of the cycle
Of birth, life, death, rebirth, redeath.
Never perfumes or gilds the self.

Comes back for you.
Perhaps right behind you.

"Keep going," he says, in his own way.

Observes a walking meditation.
Does not hurry, or drive cars or trucks.
Or tanks or gunships or warplanes.

Will not touch money or liquor.
Is beyond the vices of lust and greed.
Focused.
Not one possession of the past matters.

Old names are useless.

Accepts every moment with equanimity.
No fear. No pain. No anger. No jealousy.
Burn him. Cut him. Shoot him. Flee him.
Free him.
It is the same.

The old riddle still applies:

"Meeting the Buddha on the road,
You can say nothing to him.
You cannot remain silent.
What do you do?"

You will destroy him to be comfortable.

Some will follow his path,
Become one with him,
Laughing at the dancing bones of Zen,

The lessons of an uncertain universe.

Snakehead

When the water is wrong
You just pick up your things,
Suck in a last breath for the old times,
And walk all the way to a new pond,
So clean you can smell it.

When everything is all right,
You gobble your neighbors up,
One at a time like a thresher in frenzy,
With a gorged, wide-mouth grin,
Blimping up until you're as long
As a line of five-dollar bills.

When we get around to it,
Your passports will be revoked:

Pisces non grata à la America.

We'll have to go back to Asia
To eat you, years from now.

On the news, they say you're
A tasty reincarnated sinner
And I wonder how *karma* works out
Like that, making a funny fish face
For my visiting niece over a bowl of sour soup.

Pla Buek

Once, a long-whiskered *pla buek*
Swam beside a young boy wading
In the muddy Mekong in 1973.
A June rainbow-made-scaled flesh,
Glistening in the afternoon sun.

"Not everyone transforms
Into a sacred *Nak*. It's a blessing,"
Noted the *pla buek* cheerily.
"But I will. You'll see!"
The boy congratulated him
Politely. It seemed right to do.

"I'll prove it to you," said the fish,
Spitting a slick nugget of pure gold
Into the surprised youth's slim hands.

"I foresee you'll need that
In another country one day.
But always remember:
A head full of wisdom
Is worth more than what?"

"A tray full of jewels,"
Replied the boy knowingly.
The *pla buek* gave a noble nod,
A regal swish and splash of tail.

"You can thank me another time,
When I've changed into all
I'm meant to be. Good luck!
Sok dee!"
With that, he swam away.

The next morning, the boy's friends
Called him to the next village over.
They were celebrating a majestic catch,
Inviting everyone they saw.
They served a delicious *gaeng pla buek*,
Marveling at the vibrant scales,
The savory flesh, tasty beyond belief.
The young boy never forgot.

In the camp two years later, he hid his gift daily.
Swallowing it, passing it, then swallowing it,
Again and again and again and again and again,
For years, out of sight of everyone, even his family,
Until he was ready
To start a real life in a certain American city,
Dreaming of a tomorrow few could chase.

Now he makes Lao food the old ways (mostly)
For young people constantly on the go.
They praise his *jaew* and *sien savanh*
Far and wide, begging for his recipes.
He doesn't share the secret spices.
He laughs politely and gives to many charities.
He's honored with awards for philanthropy.
He's free.
His children think he's boring.
They never understand why
He never eats a single catfish dish.
Once a year, he reminds them,

"Be happy, but be humble. Never brag
About the great people you're going to be,
Even if it's true."
They stare at him
As if he's from outer space.

They snatch their allowance and go fishing
For the American Dream with loud laughs
And a "*Sabaidee*!"

The Last War Poem

I tell you, this is the last word for this war.
This little side war we were the center of.
There is no justice from poetry -
Any veteran can tell you that.

They want their land, their lives,
Their livestock back.

Grenade fishing in the aftermath of Phou Pha Thi
Has lost its novelty
To the man with a bullet fragment rattling
In his body, slowly tearing him apart.

"Write," they tell me. Write what?

We lost; we were forgotten; we are ghosts.
We are victims of fat tigers and foreign policy.

There is no Valhalla, only memories of Spectre gunships.
There is no Elysium, only pleas for asylum.

This jungle was filthy.

There was shit. There was blood.
There were refugees
Who, to this day, cannot explain why they were the enemy
When the war came.

Their sons fought. Their brothers died.

Their uncles, maimed, were hauled, screaming,
Into the shadows of the Plain of Jars.

"Write," they tell me, "so people won't forget.
So someone will know."

Lift the broken bodies with my words. Bring them out
And say, "We did not die in vain."

For every bullet hole, let there be a word
To stand as a monument.

For every lost limb, let there be a sonnet
To stitch the truth back together.

For every eye gone blind, let there be something
To take its place.

Something. Anything.

How can you not have words for the war of whispers?

How can you not shout, now that the whispering is done?

And I swear,
Each time I break this promise, that the next time
Will be the last word I write about this damn war.

Nakology

Not every corpse
Washed ashore
Met their ends

By a feisty *Nak* fed up
With fools frolicking
In sacred waters,

Splashing and trysting
In Vang Vieng or elsewhere,
Between hits of weed
And *Ya Ba* drama.

Fear? No,
A healthy respect is advised.
Some tragedies simply have
No magic to them.

But, once in a while,
The river returns a drained body,
Bloated but bloodless.
Silenced mouths stripped of every tooth.
It is the stuff of local whispers.
Forensics fails to comfort families.

Somewhere, some dream
Of a realm of tranquil waters cleansed.
Draconian waves of the "Other Eden."
They could lie here an eternity
In their splendid city,

Stargazing immortals
Of pitiless eye.

No Such Phi

Mae asks why I
Write of new ghosts
For our old country,
One warm night in Ceres.

"Haven't we enough
From the last seven centuries
To keep us busy?"

"Hospitality?" I reply,
Sipping a hot Ovaltine.

"Hospitality for *phi*?
Don't be silly," she says,
Smacking my head,
Returning to cook
For the coming company.

I go back to my notebooks,
Amassed over a decade:
Musings and mentions
Of suspect spirits, spooks
And ambiguous entities
We classify as *phi*.

In our majority, we burn
Our dead with some ceremony.

But it is not wholly implausible
To imagine a leathery Lao zombie,
Loathsome and lonely,
Estranged from home.

Will we dub it a *Zomphi*
Or merely *Phi Zom*?
The final nomenclature
Will be strictly academic
Amid actual panic.
You'll see.

Stout Aunty Tui insists her son,
Callow face buried in the pale
Of another mindless game,
Is the type to truly herald
The end of our meek world.

She laughs, a loud, bright Macaw,
But it is not even half as cathartic
As she hoped.

If there is an irate *Phi Kowpoon*,
Pissed at murderous noodle sellers,
It surely stands to reason
There is at least one snarly *Phi Pho*.
Although, what her precise issue is,
No one seems to know.

Uncle Som somberly suggests avoiding her,
No matter how tempting the steaming soup
Or all of her exotic condiments of lament.
Never follow her into a dark kitchen.

"That's just asking for it," he says sourly,
Adding, "Absolutely never, ever request seconds."

Regrettably, I have some doubts
Regarding my dear nephew Ninh's
Suggestion of the shocking *Phi Kachu*,
(Not to be confused with the *Phi Kasu*,
All anguished nocturnal beauty and

47

Floating melancholy viscera, etc.)
I asked him, "Do you want to get us sued?"

His petition for the awful *Phi BJ*,
Who reeks like a gooey kid's sandwich,
Oozing, smacking ghostly lips
Caked with stale peanuts and jelly,
Won't make it into the final book,
Most likely.

Still, there is a *phi* for almost everything,
Everyone.

Sometimes, new *phi* come into being with
A novel invention, such as the *Phi Tolasup*,
Haunting those who violate telephones.
Between shrill screams of white noise and static,
Their dire warnings to reform are always cut off
At the critical mo -
Leaving you hanging as *karma* approaches.

My sister Rote contemplates *Phi Bombies*,
Impolitic as it and B-52 memories may be.
We could talk all day of such legacies,
The foreign ores of war, wind and fire dug in
For four decades, bristling with secrecy.

"But at least we got a visit from Hillary."

My long-lost brother is back this year.
We ponder missing moments between us
And chuckle at the unlikely *Phi Nuckawi*,
Once beloved as the eyes of our wise city,

Departed poets who said something enduring
No one listened to.

Kinnaly

So many days in flight, in the air or on stage.
Lately, you seem half-human, half-bird,
Almost mythic, always beautiful and magic.

Bridging worlds beyond words and page,
Where trees have a special music and cities special poetry,
We pass on our hopes one song, one note, at a time,
Until, one day,

Every sword is set aside happily to build, instead,
A nation of peaceful students bright as summer lightning,
Whether in Washington or Vientiane, Paris or the Bay.

We grow, step by step and smiling,
Not just to remember today,
But to transform before returning to the heavens,

Holding the dreams of great elders and our own as one,

Not just for the world made by yesterday,
But for the best stars yet to be.

Silosoth's Secret Roads to Himapan

Read carefully:
There are at least seven secret roads
To fabled Himapan Forest through timeless Laos
Since the nights before Lane Xang and Fa Ngum.

Several routes beyond these are known, some unique,
Opening to a certain watchful eye when the stars are right.
At least one follows the flow of a sacred river.
One lurks within a fractured island full of fear.
Another, a secluded beach of bleached bones you know
By behemoth buzzards and a dancing ocean of acid.

If you take the journey, bring provisions, seek wisdom.
Be prepared to wander a lifetime.
It is beyond belief how easily you can get sidetracked
Before you even reach the gateless gate.

Suspend assumptions and ego, anchoring you
To ordinary worlds without escape, missing exits
Plain as a fragrant *dok champa* by the same road
Of profound old Buddhas and young *Nak* princes,
Crafty farmers, lovely *Kinnaly* and compassionate vets.

There are no signs to assure you and many leaps to make.
Squeezing through caverns, drinking from strange wells,
Someone has been at least that far before, once, seeking.
But doubt is a poisoned golden dagger, honed for you,
A jade cup of surrender and apologies in 10,000 tongues.

Curiosity can sustain.
A good laugh might summon a brave *Vanon* with time
To point part of the way, if they aren't full of mischief
Laughing like Xieng Mieng or some green koala.

Hermits and hunters have found hidden nooks and vales.
True lovers can spot the easiest of trails, but there are trials:
Horrific titanic elephants and saber-toothed catfish.
Nefarious *Nyak* loiter with bad maps and empty bellies.
Riddles meant for heroes and heroines are labyrinths
There are no true words for.

But if you really arrive, they shall sing songs of you.
Some might offer you the wild heart of a lotus to eat,
Or a delicious dish of *sukara-maddava* best avoided.
You might be entranced by a wondrous *Naree Pon*.
Some will challenge you, convinced you will not stay.
Others want to judge you at the holy peak of Mount Meru,
Claiming even Phou Ngeun Kailath cannot save you.

You cannot catalog the many wandering in these woods:
One leg, two legs, three legs, four legs, five legs,
Six legs, seven legs, eight legs, infinitely more, or none.
Some with wings, with hooves, or the strangest toes,
Tentacles, tusks, talons, or tendrils for your tales.
Some part bird, part stag, part "fish" or kraken.
Some part cloud, part *kirin*, part elephant or lean lion.
Some part star, part rhino, or part thundering horse.
Some part cow, part dog, part cat, or part cranky crab.
Some part crocodile, part *Nak*, or part frail human.
Some part learned monkey, part ram, or part slime.
Some part fungus, part bug, part squamous snake.
Some part tyger, part white rabbit, or part quirky rat.
Some are all of the above, or none.

Some stay the same like living mountains
Who walk or stumble.
Others are never met the same way twice.

You can ask them their true name.
Once in a while, they'll give it to you.

You can ask some for a ride back,
Or a ride forward.
There might be a price, in any case.

Incidentally, if you make it after all we've said,
There is a simple *sala* in one quiet corner,
Where you can rest your head
For a moment.
If you peek closely, you might find a certain name,
And a last bit of advice before you finish your adventure.
Laos is; Laos was; Laos will be,
But, sometimes, you will not recognize it,
Or your eternal self,
Returning to cosmic cycles to begin again,
Unless you

Passa Falang

En route to our cafe rendezvous
On University Avenue
Debating "Sushi, pho, or nachos?
Everything bagels or decadent croissants?"
Famished literary ninjas crammed in a car
(Or were we roaming gung-ho samurai?),
Pondering our ink-filled avatars,
The verbose madame from Phnom Penh
Who loves to sing, "Domo Arigato, Mr. Roboto,"
And every stanza of "Bohemian Rhapsody" at karaoke,
Reminds me, "Sabaidee will always be a foreign word."

Aloha, America. Of thee I sing.

The Dream Highway of Ms. Mannivongsa

She's still on the run in
Her dreams, but, for now, let's call her
More than Jane Doe or a number.
A number is not justice.
A name is rarely owned, mostly borrowed
In the waking world, mostly mangled
If it's more than one syllable.
And even then, that's not a guarantee.

I.

She typically begins in Cali with a "*Sabaidee*,"
Somewhere on the coast a friend calls "cerulean."

Sometimes, the surf will show up
With something for her, using a name she doesn't know.

One night, a box, a bottle, a plastic pig from Hong Kong.
Next, it's a can of worms, snakes disguised as peanuts,
A little laughing girl courier named 'Psycho Phamm'
Who wants her to go to Lansing. Or was it Lane Xang?
Maps are useless here because everything's fluid,
There one moment, gone another

Between slippery
Warps and folds.

Following blacktop only gets her as far as
Prince Sithong's legendary Ocean of Acid.

Or the Vientiane-Thai with a bunch of grad students
Debating if it's better to take a road trip or to fly
To the real House of Blues with Ajahn Xai.
She'll tell them, whatever they choose,

"First, ask your parents."

American ghosts are annoying out here.
Just ask Mrs. Winchester, or camp out by Big Sur,
Beyond the city lights, the Valley,
Or certain corners of F-No.
It feels like they're always in your damned hair.

Especially when you're looking for a big bowl of *pho*.

II.

Roundabouts have nothing on her highway.
Try to take her *tuk-tuk* the same way twice.
One time, you get to Vegas; another, you're in Reno,
Watching a man on a train rolling his life away.

Phantoms of Truth linger with the Saint of Vice.
Virtue is as easy to find as a good bookstore,
Or the fabled One-Dollar Buffet.
There is no *wat Lao* to go get married by Ajahn Elvis.

When she tries to find her friends, there's Vegas Vic
And a lady hawking deep-fried twinkies with a wink.
There's no need for education, sang the elephant in pink.
But Ms. Mannivongsa ignores most of them today.

Such as the space coyote who insists he knows her father,
A forgotten hero of the Dance Dance Revolution,
But doesn't know how the old man likes *tom mak hung*.
(The answer is: "Dirty." So dirty, it makes most men sick.)

Also, apparently, if you snub space coyotes,
Moonbeasts stalk you like a reincarnated JFK.

III.

Once in a while, like a rabbit with a bad sense of direction,
She finds herself back in Roswell, thanks to that turn
In Albuquerque, and she'll swear, every time,
They need better signs.

Feeling like a dork,
She remembers there's a bachelorette party
Where she could sing of *dok champa* gardens in bloom,
In another country more butterfly dream than gray memory.

She remembered Los Alamos just fine but not
The *axolotl* poem by Arthur Sze,
Or why "*Traduttore, traditore*"
Is an accepted way to betray, among the literary.

The local fungi taste funny.
Why, she cannot precisely say.

IV.

Zombie Kabuki in Seattle.
It's all the rage.

They love their coffee in this city,
But she recalls the snakes and bombies,
And dilapidated dinosaur museums of old Savannakhet,
Whenever she idles through.

"How many battles did it take to write the Art of War?"
She debates with the foxy lady
Who's secretly a black magic woman born to bewilder,

Like a bard's imperfect actor upon the stage
Or a stone-faced troll beneath a bridge
No gruff goat has ever known.

The world has its Wendigo, Shoggoths and Jabberwocky,
But winged *Kinnaly* remain aliens to a galaxy
Hammering a new apocalypse
For beautiful children who will grow up strangers
To the inked page,
To bricks, to mortar, to boundaries.

If she had kept the first *camera obscura* of Mozi,
Ms. Mannivongsa might have changed the cosmos,
But what is an attachment to memories
Or all of these shiny electric brains?

She prefers the dance of the mermaid and the monkey,
Free from modernity.

V.

Ha.

If you can't laugh while running.
You might as well stop now.

Ms. Mannivongsa watched the women
Weaving in the camps at Ban Napho.

Some tried remembering
Old, old promises, the trickster Xieng Mieng.

Others pondered
The wisdom of Solomon, the crows of Dumbo.
Maybe,
If her life were an opera, it would be
One part *Turandot*, one part *Pagliacci*,

Maybe a bit of *Carmina Burana*
Belting out "O Fortuna"
When she's naughty.

Psycho Phamm has her own tunes,
Half-death rattle, half-buzzard cackle,
Bone Machine variations for going out west.

In Montpelier, they dream of mountains,
Of *khaeng* and smoky synchronicity,
The riddles of Manola and her doting father,
The *dharma* of melting ice.
After midnight, there might be a knock at the window,
Someone from a lifetime ago you knew this lifetime, too.
Someone with a present for some teeth and hair,
Borrowed just for a mote of time.

Something solid that is not stone.
Gone before certain gates close again by dawn.

VI.

Down in the bayou, there are many delta *phi*
Among *loup garou* and gators, swamp things.
The mangrove and weeds under atomic skies.
Hungry *Loa* and Mississippi dreams.
Ghosts of Katrina and Versailles, debris.

Local leeches do not all glitter, but many speak French.
Others pine for blood, teats of youth, or zydeco rock & roll.
Buddhist *preta* yearn for even a single grain of rice,
Observing, morose, wailing,
<<*Laissez les bons temps roulez.*>>

With half the heart they used to have for the occasion
And no one to pray to.

Melancholy Louis mentioned to Ms. Mannivongsa
Meister Eckhart's meditations. He was so hard to
decipher:"We know so many things, but we don't know
ourselves."

"Go into your own ground.
  Learn to know yourself there."

"Only the hand that erases can write the true thing."
The Meister insisted mysteriously, cryptic as oceans.

But Louis' fragrant madeleines and marmalade
Made for a memorable morning on a riverboat queen.

American werewolves have it lucky. Their curse is a cycle.
Lao shapeshifting is a dilemma 24/7, constantly consuming
Every chance you get, humanity
A savory casino of roulette and craps.
Slaked on wayward prey,
A tiger today,
A neighbor tomorrow.
Thieves of lives, there can be no romance of their *karma*,
As if a crimson Martian god of war held perpetual sway.
The truth is a red fang full of venom.

Or a cage in a burning three-ring circus.

P.T. Barnum says, "There's a sucker born every minute."
Please, come see the egress.

VII.

She adores the ravens of Texas,
Whether Promethean, Plutonian,
African, or European,
With their tropical carrion luggage.

59

Near Dallas, she spies cat heirs of flying tigers
Who happily invite her to a slick bowl of black tea
At a hillside *café* near a memorable book depository.

Ms. Mannivongsa knows a man in Arlen
Who hates being asked if he's Chinese or Japanese
By rednecks who have no understanding of oceans,
Of secret wars and proxy armies, or refugee nations.
His wife makes apple pies to die for.

They ask when she'll have kids, every time.
Tell her to find a nice man, settle down, be happy.
They take her to karaoke after dinner,
Where she sometimes runs into an old snake who swears
He was once a man, insisting he'll switch back with a kiss.
Suddenly, she's sitting instead with a cussing horny toad
On the lone prairie.
Shooting blood from ruby eyes with no apologies,
He indulges a taste for mosquitoes and horseflies,
Whispering with breath of antique mesquite,

"Fifty years from now, no one will see any difference
Between J.R. and JFK, or who shot them.
Now, flee."

VIII.

"*Schlemiel*! *Schlimazel*! Hasenpfeffer, Incorporated!"
Ms. Mannivongsa heard, more than once, surely,
Trying to make her dreams come true, her way.

She discovers the end of history overrated,
Boxed between German walls and bamboo curtains,
Oyster worlds and Moon River crab harmonies.
To sleep, perchance to fan,
Like old Fa Ngum of his future grandson,

Whose name was writ on water.

The premise of a hyperosmiatic memory
Smells fishy to her. Suspect and useless.
But doesn't that apply to all searches
For lost time to a refugee in every life?

Lucid dreaming, waking dreams, she resorts
To imagination to cordon off traumas, broken
Promises, deferred destinies exploding on vines,
Or buried in muddy craters of Phonsavan.

If you're lucky, the Buddha will show you
Having nothing is having everything
And having everything is nothing.

It seems semi-circular, a Zen hydra
Pretending to be an ouroboros,
A generous green snake woman
Serving three cups of tea.

Milwaukee.
One day,
Cannibal City,
The next, a happy day, here again,
But not quite back where she started from.

Standing pensively on National Avenue,
Every Laostaurant does volcano chicken differently.
One constantly screws up the *khao nio*,
But, before she can speak, a giant spider invasion
Interrupts her com ....

IX.

"Denial is a river through the maze of choices,
You know," Seth suggested slyly from a spring shadow

On Setthathirat Street, slinking off to a distant dune
Like clockwork.

Midnight, digging in the garden of her mind,
She falls through to a jasmine underground
Where a smoldering soul train waits.
Many worn-out weremachines loiter here.

What the red-hot engine really burns
Is best forgotten, but "the original owners
Don't have any use for them, anymore,"
Assures her candid conductor
Between bites of spicy screwcake.

If she read the signs properly,
The bonetracks can take her to Detroit,
To gilded Dis, or dreary Youdu,
Just in time for dim sum
With her peripatetic auntie Mali
And her thousand smiles.

High above, the star kraken Ya-Sathoth
Contemplates taking the name 'Renee'
Between summons to destroy worlds
By jilted necromancers who should know better.

Ms. Mannivongsa tries to get a ticket
To take her to Laotown, but everyone she talks to
Is as helpful as the Buddha of Dropping Things
In a Chattanooga china shop.

"Watch your caboose,"
She tells a lost pooka named 'Harvey'
Looking for a party in Paris.
Or was it the Emerald City?

He thanks her with a bumblebee key.

X.

Mark the spot:
Tim Yu in Madison will mention
The second-best Chinese restaurant is Fugu,

"But do watch your pronunciation,
Though this may or may not really bug you."
He offered her *15 Chinese Silences.*
Besides *"Khop jai lai,"* what could she say?

Ms. Mannivongsa likes to call her sister Phet
On International Talk Like A Pirate Day,
Or when she gets dreams of giant catfish
Frolicking in the dank caves of Vang Vieng,
Or an alleged ragged edge of allegorical Elgin.

A cocky skinwalker sits nearby, occupied
Spilling his coffee on a cheap copy of
*Skimming an Anthology of Chinese Poems
Of the Dang Dynasty* he barely understands,
Any more than the shrugs of Ayn Rand,
Or how to rage against machines.
He thinks he governs all he surveys,
But he's just a puppet of iron pyrite,
Defanged before he could really bite.

The opulent *sala* at the Olbrich Botanical Gardens
Is a treasure of the city. Most are an exercise
In modesty in the old country, a respite for tired feet.
But you rarely run into eldritch architectural philosophy
In the race to erect titans of glass and concrete,
Their mouths elevators, their stomachs gray cubicles,

Slowly digesting you one report, one ring at a time
Until you're some sad, wandering *phi* sobbing in a hall,
Seen only by a security camera no one monitors.

XI.

Rats live on no evil star:
Good luck in China, pests in New York,
Especially in the walls.

Last time in the city, some sleazy Hee-Haw reject
Was threatening to take his Texas time with her,
"Every way but wrong," arrayed in tacky rhinestones.

When she's awake, magic doesn't usually work right,
But, sometimes, *karma* lends a hand or calls a cab,
Conveniently.

A poet friend, back from practicing
His mad science in Imperial City,
Had a day off and went to an aquarium,
Marveling at dolphins and *jiang kui*,
Wondering if we're evolved remoras, secretly.

At night, she never goes without her six-demon bag
She found for a steal in Little China, ten times more handy
Than crappy designer knockoffs her friends tote absurdly.

Doc Ratsabout asks in the shadow of Lady Liberty,
"Was King Kong secretly a *Vanon* veteran?
A sulking simian sword-saint
Who somehow survived
The savage siege of Lanka

With the honored hero Hanoumane,
Living out the last of his modest pension
Pent up on Skull Island?"

Yank someone from his home
Just for a sideshow, you can't expect
Everything will be dandy.

She debates which souvenirs to get her niece in Modesto.
The official Trippy Master Monchichi, or Hello, Piggy?
A rare copy of *It Ain't Truth If It Doesn't Hurt*, maybe?
Wayward Wah-Ming would know,
But she's always busy in a library,
Or off wandering a street of albino crocodiles.

That's the persistent problem with this city:
Who ya gonna call?

Her cousin Noy is right: Some have an angel heart.
But those were usually in a jar on their desk, waiting
For the girl of
Their dreams.

How could she ever live here, when it was so hard
To find a decent bowl of *kowpoon*?

XII.

Sweet home, Chicago,
Windy "Hog-butcher for the world":

In the early years of foggy hope, you could catch
A show by Silavong Keo and the Strangers,
Or maybe see Voradeth Ditthavong croon a tune

Like "Kid Tung Nang" for a little change.

Ms. Mannivongsa felt bad for Minnie the Moocher,
Who liked to slum around Chinatown
With big dreams of the King of Sweden,
Until they took her away, mad as a March hare.

She arrived by meditating on tangerine dreams
And the risky business of love on a real train,
Hands that rock cradles and giant peaches.
She was tired of everyone wanting to rule worlds.

A man with a blue guitar invites her to Iowa
To teach her about Tikbalang stogies and ghost wars.
He was a down-to-earth go-to guy who'd been there.

But first, she'd have to figure out how
To change her shape back into a human
Before the Silence arrived
On more than little feet.

XIII.

Cats in Philly.
Some can walk through walls.
Others are surely from Saturn.
Some are filled with fleas, or Napoleons of Crime,
Out of the bag like a fashionable Houdini.

Yes, Lao help put the *phi* in Philadelphia,
But the place had plenty of its own spirits to start.
Just go to the library and ask that boxer, the haunted vet,

Or Adrienne Su, who will tell you,
Miss Chang is missing.

There's a mother who will inform you
She was once an undercover cop in Vientiane,
Even though she couldn't keep a secret today
To save her life. But she cooks a mean barbecue.
A word of advice: Never try to beat her at cards.

They celebrate Pii Mai Lao in the streets in April,
When the moon is full and a year of memories is made.

Some years,
You think of ancient Gop Nyai, hungry for moons.
Or a king and his riddles, his thirst for heads and vows,
Blood to bless a parched land, seven beautiful daughters,
And a clever young boy who eavesdrops on talking birds.

Ms. Mannivongsa typically wonders,

Where was the queen this whole time?
But people just stare at her like Horse-Face Keo.

XIV.

One blue moon, a tiny ant climbed onto her chest
Before Ms. Mannivongsa started dreaming,
Heavy as castle stone.

She couldn't move an American inch
In the darkness of her creaking Ceres home.

"Don't tell me you don't recognize your own
Grandmother," the ant began with a tsk.

"I'm here to warn you: Change your ways
Or you'll join me building anthills in an afterlife."

"Are you sure you're really my grandma?"

"If I am, I should probably do something
About my complexion," the ant replied, leaving
For a distant field of cinders and screams
Starting to miss her.

XV.

Sometimes, she's back in traction.

Or one of the flesh cobblestones of croaking hell
For rolling ratkings of filth and limbs entwined,
Punished for avaricious abuses of another life,
Yet not quite meriting a dirty boot stomping
A human face forever for reality TV.

Someone slipped her a note in the factory,
In the 1980s: *I LOVE YOU.*
But where could that have gone
In this new world?
She'd seen enough of where this went
For one lifetime, already.

There were so many unsatisfying little deaths.
Why would she take a chance
With romance in a tongue
That would never truly be

Hers and hers alone?

At least her *karma* was.

XVI.

No one ever cares who she is, when she's awake.
Until the night she remembers her dreams.

"Do you remember who you are?"
It is not merely what pursues that haunts.

She hates the lady who convinced her
For so many years she was so much less
For reading ahead. For reading at all.
What becomes of such bitter creatures?

But the monks just tell her to let go.

Attachments are a thorny road to the infernos
Of Nalok. Perhaps the hell of black thread
Or the screaming hell of hot tridents.

Ever since the accident,
She's been uncertain
She made it, in reality.

What if she was now just a figment
Of a poet's imagining of a *nuckawi*,
Trying to preserve someone she loved
But could not name?

She doesn't remember every place
Everyone tells her belongs to her,
As if it can never be taken away.

She smiles, trying to share their certainty.

XVII.

She's doesn't know if her friend thought it through,
Remembering her grandfather the old ways,
Burning paper call girls and cell phones
But not batteries or contracts good in the afterlife.
It's just as well.

Who's the first person he would really call every hour
With the demands of an old man with paper prostitutes?

Ms. Mannivongsa told her niece resentfully,
"They make you sound crazy
If you can remember your past lives.
They write you off if you say you were Napoleon.
Everyone says they're Napoleon or Caesar.

"No one cares if you're a big nobody,
A minor also-ran to Genghis Khan:
Schlubby Shan Yu-meets-Walter Mitty
Or a klutzy half-wit lieutenant of Yoshitsune.

"Buddha help you if you remember
Waking up a roach again
Or a time-traveling scorpion."

Some daughters of Da Nang see
A generous rabbit in the moon,
But, born south of Luang Prabang,
Ms. Mannivongsa was taught while young
There's a stranded grandmother and a little girl,
Because they had one last chance at immortality
For all of humanity, but botched the question
When an idle god walked by.

Her mother scolded every year,
"When shooting moon-munching frogs,
Be careful. Don't get Grandma and the girl
In the crossfire. Drunks forget,
But you know better."

"Can't someone just grab a ladder?"

"It doesn't work that way, anymore."

XVIII.

A few minutes earlier, she was on the Bolaven Plateau,
But now it might be the Roof of the World.

Red-faced Yama the Dharmapala, on vacation from Hell
With an elder frogman, Mr. Finnegan from St. Paul,
Discussed demon kings who disavow paths of pain
To protect profound truths of the souls' labyrinths.

Passing time debating tigers and butterflies,
They pondered,

"Who was truly the most dangerous?
The intentional or the reckless?
Who they were, or what they might become?"

They offer Ms. Mannivongsa a cup of cold butter tea,
Appraising her like a bloody rice cake.

She remembers
The century she accidentally ate a ghost's food.
For decades, they never let her forget for a minute.
But she learned you can stop some ghosts with a fishnet,
More often than a promise.

Especially a pledge to return.

XIX.

Ms. Mannivongsa wept.

In the court of the Toad King Khankhaak,
She expected old wart stories
Of the time he raised an army
Against peevish Thaen

Over disputed rain and the slights of men.
He told them to anyone who would still listen.

He was no help against hungry frogs
Hunting her.

But he was nice enough to offer
Ant egg soup for her trouble.

Deep down, she wished she'd gone
To visit the Chameleon Prince instead,
As Psycho Phamm suggested.
On Earth, kindly Mae Thorani
Demonstrated how to easily
Wash fat demons right out of her hair.

XIX.

Here comes purple rain, yellow rain, acid rain, again.
Someone set it all afire over the Land of 10,000 Lakes,
North American troll territory, filled with libraries.
And tinkering gremlins.

"You should come see my paradise of bombs,"
She said to the nice bluesman with the ox-head,
As she stepped off the green bus by the capital.

He offered to take her to see Styx at Mystic Lake.
But she forgot to get his number as he drove away,
Taking his pokey pal with the face of a grass mud horse
To the cinema at the Great Mall of America:
The Great Old Gatsby Goes To Woebegotcha.

C'est la vie, babe.

Ms. Mannivongsa found Mae Nak

In a chilly Frogtown basement off Minnehaha,
Pounding away at a dish of *tom mak hung*
With a teak pestle and her bowl of hard clay.

She was short of lime and fresh crab.
But everything else was pungent and powerful,
From *padaek* to ghost peppers and green papaya.
Her secret was using *Fantomes du Laos*,
Tomatoes said to glow when spirits stop by.

"Never let death hold you back,"
She advises, offering Ms. Mannivongsa a taste.
How delicious it was!

Up by Minnetonka,
Mad Mark Willcox loves to tell
Ms. Mannivongsa tall tales
Of the unanticipated, such as
Trembling Camp Wolfeboro tenderfeet
Who dread the Calaveras County Monster.
"People wander all of the time," he reminds her.
"It doesn't mean they're lost."

Beneath a silver moon, she dreamt
Of ornery Peg Powler against
Sapphic vampyres of humane intent
And lady lycanthropes of Wolf's Point.
No matter who wins, someone will drown
Their sorrows, a Mississippi of tears.

A legendary poetess from Hell
Might walk away with a haiku,
An ode to frame the times.

Will she sing of punk *phi*,
Hungry for cool jerks,
The mumbling fiends of MonstroCity,

Or lost boy DJs and learned *naiku*
Of a Neverland burlesque?
No one cares as much about
Big trouble in Little Champassak,
Or the pending showdown
In the shadows of Laotown,
The unlocked gates to Nalok,
Or the one-way express to Avici.

Once, dining with the Lady of the Mekong,
She learned crying doves taste like chicken.
Thankfully, not lutefisk.

XX.

Ms. Mannivongsa's friends Soysauce and Gai
Pester her persistently: "Get away in Murfreesboro!"

There, she has a chance to watch
The morning news with Uncle Chantho,
Or listen to a new Alonzo Silavong song
During a tasty weekend Laobecue at Pon and Oudone's.
Mr. Farmer was almost done building a nice house,
But he was almost worn down to a lingering bone.

By an old Civil War cemetery,
The monks have a *wat* for the Lao community.
Wandering cats and puppies keep you company
With a Tennessee *sabaidee*.

Lao elders drop out of the sky for festivals,
Or dance like monkeys from the old country.
Eddie says everyone's ready for zombies.
Even ghouls.

Maybe an angel or two.

It was all so tempting,
A green mango for a long, long road.

XXI.

"Frogs are the original refugees,"
Her mother insisted, making steamed *mok gop*.
"One life in sea, one life on land, thinking it's safer,
But the old ones know the truth. No such safety.
There's always danger everywhere,
Especially if you're stupid and forgetful."

"It's okay to be kind. Be as kind as you can.
But don't be stupid. Never be stupid.
Memories you're meant to keep find you again.
Wisdom, not so much."
Some nights, her parents got drunk and bickered.
At 2am., her mother would come into the bedroom,
Crying in the dark to her and her sister.
"Your daddy is a hero to strangers, not to your momma.
Not to your momma," she'd say,
Reeking of smoke and tequila.

"It's okay. He's not your real daddy, you know.
You always know.

"Your father is a *Nak*,
A *Nak* prince from Valusi, far beneath the sea.
Someday, he come back for you, for me. He take me away.
He promised. When everything is ready. I'll be happy."

Other nights, she stormed in, angry as a red-faced elephant,
And she'd rant, "Not my daughter, not my daughter.
You're not."Your real momma a bullfrog. A big, fat, ugly
bullfrog.
Look just like you.

"She didn't want to keep you; she give to me.
You not lucky. You not special. Go to your real home.
You can go be stupid there,
Until you get eaten up like your momma.

"Why are you acting like a human?
Turn back into what you really are!
Go! Go!"

Ms. Thammavongsa hated those stupid jokes.
Hated those stories. Hated being a stranger everywhere.
Didn't ask for this. Didn't ask for anything.
And what help was her sister?
Drinking dessert with her, she'd tease,
"Why are you drinking frog eggs?
They could be your real sisters!
Are you a cannibal? Are you a cannibal?"
Ms. Thammavongsa doesn't eat a thing
With tapioca beads, anymore. She lost a taste for it.

Her sister wonders why she never calls.
"If you don't have family, you don't have anything,"
Ajahn Anan says, every time she visits the *wat* to pray.

XXII.

Maak ngu gin hang is a game:
"Snake biting the tail."
You win if the head closes the circle
And nothing falls apart, hanging onto
Each other for dear life.

Pyscho Phamm loves to play.

XXIII.

Her family.

They tried to get her help
The usual ways.

Interventions. Rehab.
Prayer circles. Scared straight.
Rigged psychic readings and tarot drawings.
Talk to the monks. Talk to the shrinks.
Talks with the teachers. Talks with the elders.
Hypnotherapy. Self-help books by smarmy gurus.
Crystals, candles and sweat lodges.
Changed diets. Changed prescriptions.
Feng shui, *vastu vidya*, hokey pokey.
You name it.

She still claws at her own skin in her dreams, this year.
It sloughs off so easily. Detaches by flakes and chunks.
Flesh is covering scales covering ... something
Beyond words.

It all floats and bobs away in bubbles and ooze towards
The center of the ocean. A cold center of the cosmos.
Wherever.

Is she a lizard? A fish? An octopus baroness?
What if she's a fateless, coffee-colored mermaid,
Or a frumpy *tanuki* for a sad tuna world?

North of Athabasca, halfway to Midian,
A few left turns near Innsmouth or possibly Arkham,
There's a short pier by a lighthouse and a cheap carnival.
Psycho Phamm introduces an old Valusian, Mayavin,
Who cracks wise that he's been many things.

One day, Merlin; another, a clever African spider.

Looking at him makes her cough up
A gout of shiny black snakes who slither away
Between the aged pier planks without one look back.

He laughs at her.
Winking an ophidian eye,

"Magic is only an illusion. Reality, another.
Family, too. Truth, even more treacherous.
Maybe I'm kidding. Would it matter,
For you to believe? Let me show you true change."

XXIV.

There's a certain library in Argentina
You can only reach these days by dreams.
The path is akin to a phantasmagoric Chartres labyrinth,
Lined with riddles everyone knows and groans over.
But, in this library, by a certain stack and a certain shelf,
Is a more straightforward road to Himapan, according
To mischievous Mayavin.

There, near any number of odd volumes, such as
The Voynich Manuscript and *De Vermiis Mysteris*,
The works of Von Juntz and Van Wormer,
There is a small sentence in a small book,
If read aloud on the right night in the right way,
Will open a gate to the holy forest.

But you can only do this once and then
Everything will change. Again.

XXV.

Old Madame Yaga likes to come count spoons
When most other people are sleeping, but she runs into
Ms. Mannivongsa frequently enough they both smile
Whenever they see each other now.

"Rodina, Mississippi, Mekong, Amazon,
All same river to simple fish like us,"
She always laughs.

"Be true to yourself, like this old babushka lady.

Live a long time; see the worlds, darling."

She snickers of the sexy *Nakh* of Estonia,
Changing shape to drown gullible rubes.
"So many tricks, for such a simple end."
She heaps scorn on such one-trick sirens.

Madame Yaga suggests to Ms. Mannivongsa,

"Visit the voluptuous *Vouivres* by the Seine.
See their lovely carbuncles with a hue of rubies.
They'll treat you like a sister in this cold life.
"You can see where this is leading, darling?"

Ms. Mannivongsa nods,
Packing some sticky rice and a one-legged hen
For Madame Yaga, but she's gone.

XXVI.

Waffle Kingdom. It's hard to choose here.
The kind of restaurant you don't plan to go to.
You just sort of end up there.
Psycho Phamm likes pancakes with spice.

"Panic cakes," she calls them with a smile.
Don't bother correcting her.

Ms. Mannivongsa is still wondering what to order
When he comes in with his swaggering retinue,
All arrayed in their fancy monkey suits,
Black bolo ties; white shirts crisp, overstarched;
Heads shaggy manes hinting of better nights.
They take seats all around the room while he
Sidles up to her after Psycho Phamm has left
To wash her decaying hands.
"Careful. You are what you eat," he jokes
With a non-committal smile of maybes and mischief.
He says his name is 'Han.'
He's been around a long, long time.

Han hardly looks human, skin orange leather
From too many days too close
To a laughing yellow sun.

They talk of strange lives, old wars.
Fears of things within and without.
Good soldiers never really dying,
Just "going back to hell to regroup."
After all, that's where they're needed most.

They laugh over human beings and human doings.

"Don't let those limits apply to you in this lifetime,
For once."

Maybe she knows why he's here.
Maybe it's too late to change what's been.
Maybe that's not going to end even if she woke up.
Maybe this is the night she feels truly alive
And she can tell herself, *I'm okay with that.*

He intimates before departing,

"Not everything that matters
Hinges on Himapan.
We need you 'here,' my dear.
"But one day, you'll see:
Crossing between stars is easy.
It's simple as a river, a room.

"Ask Old Zeno, if he gets here.
He knows better than anyone."

They stiffed her with the bill.

Psycho Phamm comes back in.

"What did I miss?"

XXVII.

One day, when all of her wars are done,
She might get to come home,
No longer on the run.
Someone might remember her true name.
They might get her a cup of coffee,
Cook something the way *mae* used to make.
Laugh about a common memory from a shared country.

What she made true, and what she did not,
Won't matter that much,

Only the one thing she's certain
To tell her friend who arrives with her,

"I'm a stranger here, myself."

Ba

From the moment I met her,
    She's been wiggling,
    Squirming,

        This way and that,
        Like a naughty young *Nak*,

    Or a baby *pla beuk*
    Who dreams of wide seas.

I'm only inviting her to visit,
My words a humble net of black line

She slips through every time.

Just when I think I've got her,

    Surprise, she's changed again into something
    Almost immortal,

Splashing in the pools of my memory,
        Swimming just out of reach,

While I stand upon the beach, laughing,
Beneath hot stars opening the door for night

And my dreams, where she's so much easier to hold onto.

Digging For Corpse Oil

We know
Rabbit's feet aren't lucky for rabbits.

The position on corpse oil seems vague
For those beyond this realm of mortal cares.

In certain lands, they're a treasure for rites
Most find too hideous to mention.
Modern medicine considers it unsanitary,
While soulless corporations have not yet found
A monetary percentage to profit by,
So it remains a cottage industry, dying off,
Dripping away, little by little, every day.

If you must know,
Not just any old body in the dirt will do.
And there's an art to desecration, if you're serious.
The 'experts' claim the body is quite multipurpose,
If you're not attached to it the way some societies are.

Certain bodies for certain things.
Dig in silence,

Until you get to your prize.
Fresh is easier to work with.
The right candle is essential, beneath the chin,
On the right night amid proper conditions.

You don't collect much from a single body but enough,
If you've been brought to this poor point in the first place.
It's not for amateurs and the penalties are stiff if caught.

Predictably, most want the oil for luck in lust.
A few want protection from their own karma,

For hanging around with the wrong crowd.
Reasons vary.

I feel sympathy for the ones who hit all of the branches
On their way down the thorny Trees of Fate:
Poor, pregnant with their first baby and murdered,
Now wandering the afterlife with a burnt chin,
While carefree high-rollers dig themselves deeper
Into dippy drama, thanks to amulets made from those
They think
"Anonymous."

Bless it all you want.
Believe in blind judges.
Behave as you will.

Perhaps the body is a stairway
More than a revolving door,

Where young children might ask,
"What's monstrous in the world, after all?"
Watching foreign refineries on the Mekong
Dig for liquid dinosaur bones,
Fuelling fancy cars for finite lives
Speeding to their next destination.

It almost sounds like a scream.

The Doom That Came To New Sarnath

*"I never ask a man what his business is, for it never interests me.
What I ask him about are his thoughts and dreams."*
— H.P. Lovecraft

After a time, you understand: Not every city is forever.
Ask Skara Brae or Irem of the Pillars,
Moldy Croatan or Macondo.

Some old folks in Fargo know a pretty fortune teller
Of unerring accuracy.
Seventh daughter of a seventh daughter,
Born beneath a blue full moon during
Gop kin deuane one Pi Mai Lao,
Just south of Salavan,
She bobbed over the borders
With the third wave.

She was a regular Laostradamus, they joked.

No one likes her much.

The limits of her powers, you see, extend only
To purple predictions of misfortune.
Tarot or I-Ching, palmistry or bibliomancy,
The end results are invariably

"Utter Doom." Or worse.

Every day, she thinks of moving,
Maybe get a regular job.
Maybe migrate to Minnetonka.

A few vermillion miles remote of the 52,
Dr. Ketmani and I drove by
Her little ramshackle on the prairie,
Lonely as a *mor lum* singer at noon,
More bubblegum-patchwork,
Broken lumber and discount paint
Than anything cozy.

Useless barbed wire sighed in the sun, wondering
Who would come by worth keeping out or keeping in.

A few postcards from madmen afar thanked her
On a tired corkboard by the creaking door.
One asked her to marry him.
He's gone now, we learned later.
Eyes of Endor hazel, hippy as a hot spring Hodag,
Hair a fresh hurricane of frayed whipcord,
She's Lao Elvira in a macabre red *sinh*,
Introducing herself as Miss Keo
With scant primping or theatricality.

It was only two.
She said, "I knew you would come."
She almost believed it.

II.

Over *laab* and *lao lao*, she's a host of better humor
Than her reputation suggests, happily dispensing
To anyone who'd listen.

Skeptics as we were,
We hedge our bets and ask of times far, far from us.
She's disappointed, but recounts the coming, trembling:

Centuries hence, the Raw Ones rise,
Wild from a thousand primal hungers,
Sour-fleshed, firm-toothed, relentless.

Faithful priests of barbed *Phra Bok: The Cleansing*
Will claim all dreaming is ended for what little remains.
By the lake near New Sarnath,
They chant in frantic Pali for deliverance.

The Melted Face and Traceless Blade
Laugh from the charred hills, merciless,
Cactus for souls, waiting for stragglers.

The ears of New Sarnath had grown deaf decades before.
Diplomacy died expediently; credit alone drove policy;
Fangless rituals of ambassadors observed strictly for show.

The eye of the city had no sense of poetry left.
Wisdom was a greater liability than the pornographic.

The holy core preferred mobile phones and good wi-fi
To *mor phi* mysticism or saffron Dhammic disciplines,
No matter how diluted.
All of their modern applications proved wholly ineffective
Against the viral surge as the first clawed through,
Hungriest for pure minds, although any morsel sufficed.

The gates of New Sarnath glistened with expensive polish,
Bristling barrels of basic death by ray, vapor, projectile,
Poised to defend, but turned on the panicked throngs
To protect politicians, preferred hedonists and sycophants,
Infected or not.
Policing is more practical in these days.

Their astrologers were no foundation of hope,
Too focused prognosticating profitable fornication
Than averting calamity or the inopportune discoveries

Of curious Victim Zero. Predictably devoured,
Unmourned.

The root and beams of promise course through the streets,
Long-rotted by decadent pseudo-clans of perverse cruelty,
Hoarding influence, corrupting process in favor of elites.
Permissive kleptocrats were worse than necromancers
Dabbling in flesh-eating bacteria and immortality.
The famished fed for days on the cornered ones,
Who could scream no law, no order in any tongue
To save their gilded heads.

The warriors were a tragic cracked crossbeam, defending
A city who no longer deserved saving, overrun, swarmed
Over, torn apart easily from their armored posts, despite
Possessing more sleek weapons than residents.
They may as well have been
A spilled crock of ant egg soup.

Honest and loyal district chiefs might have been
A golden wall where a different destiny unfurled,
But they were burnt in the furnaces long ago,
Baked into petty bourgeois bio-char briquettes,
Fueling a clumsy circus of mirrors insatiable for power.
Perhaps they were the lucky ones.

The ministers of surveillance had abandoned their posts,
Bored of watching gamblers and vice, boundaries of justice
Too fluid to take seriously, desensitized to atrocity.
It was no surprise they did not recognize real danger.
They saw nothing they understood, even at the last,
As the Abyss reached for them,
A long-lost brother from Avici.

Merchants and entrepreneurs were sure of their futures.
Without their prosperity, the city would be senseless!

They taught their brilliant ways of purchase, all mere
Commodities to exchange and barter, even souls.
Aliens paid the best, especially for the unrefined.

What the traders gave each other as New Sarnath died
Was of no lasting matter when the Raw Ones finished,
Demonstrating true greed, one frenzied bite at a time.

Elders used to say the heart of a city was measured by its
physicians and pretty princesses. As they ran the labyrinth,
Impossibly beautiful even in its last cursed hours, the heart
Learned what it truly loved and lost, every sense afire.
Tears fell,
Knowing nothing would escape or remember.

New Sarnath, once squandered, wildly ascending.
Ores torn, forests burnt, citizens ground heedlessly.
Now naught remains but the wasted ruins of fools.
The clouds of the city drift to other realms,
Guardian spirits of old, once mocked, depart,

Hard raindrop shadows above a cracked neon street.

To Relatives I Never Knew

I.

By Sanzu, by Styx,
Or a nascent Laotian rivulet,
I pray, to whoever is in charge of such things,
That after a turbulent lifetime
On these teeming banks,
Crowded as the ashen Ganges,
We will recognize each other,
Indeliberate strangers that we were,
And understand.

II.

Beneath a cleansing icon of lovely Mae Thorani

With what passes for new family for a new land,
She rumbles to an obscure saint of speculation

"Maybe you were all petty demons in a past life
  I swept away without a strain, a thought."

Filthy, nameable, mere, finite among the infinite

One fine winter in the tropics before a Nak prince
Was reborn as Buddha.

III.

The Drowning God keeps busy.

He has an ocean of second-hand memories
No one gets to see.

His fluid voice smothering,
He pretends he can never hear you
Amid the many worlds' tears.

Nakanya

Brings true wealth, wisdom, a gift of secrets,
And stories for worlds yet to be.

Some say she is the daughter of Lady of the Mekong.
Others claim her in different legend: a princess, a dragoness
Near fragrant rivers of potters and dreamers,
Gilded caverns and underground grottos heroines tread.

Nakanya brought a pearl worth 3,000 galaxies before
An assembly of bodhisattvas, a present for the Buddha.
Knowing her potential, he accepted her boon on Vulture Peak.

"Watch: I now shall become a Buddha," she said,

"Even faster than a present can be accepted."
This she accomplished in a heartbeat
Heard across the cosmos.
"What is beyond anyone, anything,
If a *Nak*'s daughter can become a Buddha?"
They now sing by the white lotus, the thickest clouds,
The five obstacles, the darkest days.

Infinite in potential, vast as the Ksheera Sagara,
A gift of a lifetime, whether an instant
Or a strange aeon.

Naklish

Hidden ideas dwell deep. Enigmatic notions.
Idly dreamt:
"Do angels read Enochian?"
Determined, I scour creation, obscure view, endless rumor.
Eventually, they entered, restoring numinous arcana like
Naklish, ancient knowledge lingering in secret hearts.

Dream

When the dream ends, it seems
I've forgotten half of the things
I said I'd remember.
Thank God it's nothing like real life.

But I'm always in a bustling city where
I'm doing something more diverting
And there, I never seem to make mistakes,
Or, at least, I don't notice

And no one
(Not even the little gnomes and rosy kappas)
Calls me out on it.

I wish I could tell you the words
I'd said that once seemed so profound
Between one and three am.
Amid the Tiger Kings
And their dying courts
To defend myself,

But all I remember
Is a broken promise

Made in color.

Into Worlds of Meaning

Alina and Alwin
Were not a modern Hansel and Gretel
Living an "American Dream" in a witch house,
Contemplating Candyland monopolies,
But they had their own stories unfolding by the day.

There was an old Sphinx who did not die
At Thebes, just because some orphan peeked
And answered her ponderous riddle about life.
She was peeved, but it wasn't the end of the road,
Let alone a world.

She wasn't stuck in one shape or another, this Sphinx,
Raging like some minotaur in an endless labyrinth.
She took to travel and peeked in from time to time
On interesting children.

Bright ones, noble friends, especially.
The kind who are okay wondering who they really are.
Who'd be terrified at an ordinary life, an easy path.

Maybe, one day, they'd reclaim Lao voices.
During an afternoon June rain, they might choose
Tales of daring Kalaket and flying Manikab
Over legends of the white Pegasus sprung fresh
From a fierce fight with serpent-tressed Medusa
In her gardens of stone.

They might say, "*Sabaidee*,"
The way others say "Open, *Sesame*,"
To open the secret doors of their lives.

They might laugh about *Vanon*,
Pondering if they were cavemen we had no names for,
Or truly monkeys scampering among the heavens.

95

Over a plate of *sien savanh* and *khao nhio*,
They might discuss grand pianos and black belts,
Fast trains and philosopher's stones,
The *khaeng* and the drake of Lake Phalen,
Memory a welcome phoenix in any tongue.

Who knows where they will go by the end,
Following the way of the foot, hand, soul, and dream

In a world where a single letter can lead to
A book or a parent's surprise,
A timely reminder of Grandma Khek,
Filled with love in a changing Laos,
Not so far away as some might think.

Notes can become gates, a strange box of hope,
A puzzle for tomorrow,

Songs splendid as a timeless *dok champa*
Among the inviting stars.

The Raja and the Salamander

Shall I tell of the mystic Mayavin or witty Xieng Mieng?
The Rakshasa Sutra or the Forgotten King?
The secret histories of Matsanari or Sisattanag
Among the Naga cities of the Mekong?

"These are fables and fantasies,
Not coin and fire," he replies idly,
With a yawn by our languid stream.

And so are we, between the merciless teeth
Of stars and memory.

Above, a blackbird circles with a raucous laugh.

Stainless Steel Nak

Like a young monk we call "Ai,"
More slippery than a rat or some diamond dog of war,

Watching bunnies clobber tigers who ate the sweet blue ox,
Full of havoc meant for Albuquerque or ambitious Betelgeuse,

Will you shrink into some chrome cobra,
                    An analog anaconda,

Or a steady horse boxed in on some Neo-Napoleonic
                                Animal farm

Dreaming of dynamite and tasty electric sheep,
                        Black as busty Kali?

Maybe it's true people are made of monkey minds or
Aimless pig heads scowling like Beelzebub among his flies,
Watching a floating green world of cock crows and denials

Yearning for bits of heaven, the honey of angels if not bills,
A world that cannot be translated as we sing the blues
Well met, remembering lone, level sands,
The mighty works.

A raven laughs like Prometheus, David unrepentant,
Yelling for Lilith more than Rachel, more than Eve,
Among all of the painted pillars of wisdom in the rain,
Coated in the cobwebs of a tiny orange spider with her
Perfect recall

Of former lives worth stealing between
                        Sanitized salutations.

In memory of Harry Harrison (1925-2012), et al.

The Spirit Catches You and You Get Body Slammed

I came to Missoula to ask him
About the inner workings of *ua neeb*.
To understand the symbolic significance of split horns
And spirit horses who trace their noble smoky path
To turns of an auspicious moon above ancient Qin.

My tape recorder at the ready,
My fountain pen freshly filled with indigo ink,
My ears, my eyes, my heart:
All were humbly waiting for
The wise shaman's words
To impart to the next generation
Of youths who sought this fading voice.

He spoke and my interpreter said,
"Who's your favorite wrestler?"

I wasn't certain I'd heard properly.

"Grandpa wants to know who your favorite wrestler is."
My interpreter turned back to the shaman, speaking Hmong.

Rising with a stately elder's grace,
The shaman confidently said,
"Randy Macho Man Savage!" and struck a macho pose.

Smiling, he then offered me a cup of hot coffee.
I was too stunned to say anything more
For the rest of the afternoon.

Years later, I still have dreams of shining Shee Yee
Smashing writhing demons into blue turnbuckles,
Watching next to a hundred smiling shamans in the
Audience.

War Kinnaly

Some scholars scold, "War *Kinnaly* do not exist."
They deny these lissome ladies were ever there
At the long siege of Lanka, let alone the skies of Troy.

I am told
They did not sit idly chirping with brother Sin Xay,
Bivouacked before battle
Among their 500 feathered cousins.

Pretty Princess Manola has never met one,
Even at the darkest edge of holy Himapan.

If you believe your teacher,
They will not ride with the Valkyries at Ragnarok,
Or among the apocalyptic armies of Armageddon,
Olive-green vultures of fluttering wing.

They did not hammer out their thundering melodies
Over the Americas in 1812.

Or screech of glories and the march of truth
In their hymns by Savannah or the halls of Montezuma.
If you trust what you've been told so far.

To hear most versions,
These divas did not mangle La Marseillaise
In the mud of Dien Bien Phu or the Rhine.
They look nothing like a whistling Artemis
Or Amazons of Paradise Island.

Who dares whine they have no appreciation
Of the *dok champa* and ravens,

Or the headless tunes of Samothrace,
Mocking old Pyrrhus and Alexander,
Warbling at wax-eared Odysseus with his Sirens.

I look at a volume of the truth of my secret wars.
Puff the Magic Dragon belches fiery lead
upon the paddies
and the people.

It is not called obscene.

Democracia

Father was a tiger
Ground beneath the wheels.

His fat was burned to light a torch,
But there's no liberty here,

Only the ashes of the village
That couldn't evolve,

Where ghost grandchildren play with ghost grandparents
And the parents are nowhere to be seen at all.

Where have they gone? Where have they gone?
A delay of a day for an idea, a delay of a lifetime

For the dead upon the ground.

Look what remains -

This hut hasn't the ambition of Ozymandias.
These craters were once a rice field.
This ox was no man's enemy.

And what we have left to say could explode any minute.

World Records

There are two Hmong
Who hold world records.
One for flying under fire,
The other for doing nothing
With his hair.

Half the time, their names aren't
Pronounced properly.

Among the things they share
In common is that both
Are dead today,
Making the slow transition
From a living room rumor over a cold beer
To a tropical legend for scholars
At the yawning border of the Dream Kingdoms.

At least one report has suggested
The Guinness Book of World Records
May shut down shop soon,
So someone else
Will have to remember this
If they think it's worth the trouble.

I wish I could remember their names,
But, sometimes, I don't even remember
Who I am, anymore.

A Sphinx Reviews Myths as Self

I.
Adopting. Growing.
Illegal alien: Son.
Truth. Justice. A way?

II.
Strong, green marvel: Heart,
You won't like me when angry.
Exploited. In love.

III.
Old man, mutt, here:
Such countless, wasted chances.
Disappointing skulls.

A Discussion of Monsters

In America, monsters arrive
Through Ellis Island,
Or from the stars,
Or morning's rogue angels.

In Asia, the ghosts hop,
Hair long, eyes black,

And girls from Taiwan will squeal in terror
At that lonely world,

But laugh with disdain
At Hollywood's soulless piles of pixels and latex,
Signifying obsolete demons.

My Body, A Span of Stars to Be

I can't sleep tonight, so I'm typing.
Old white men suggest
The incessant sensations
Of something writhing within
Are simply cancers taking root,
Or perhaps vicious, virulent parasites,
But nothing special we haven't seen before.
They keep you humble that way.

"These are alien only to you,"
Is the height of their reassurance.
Certain Lao suggest if it gets
Really bad, perhaps it is a *Phi Pob*
Possessing me, devouring me from
The inside and, by the time it's done,
Every gut shall be a corrupted shred
And everything I've said will be read
Like the ravings of a lunatic best burned.
But there's an herb for that.

At a subatomic level, I know I'm 99.9%
Nothing, so I'm not certain what anything
Is latching onto, but what's solid, if it
Collides fast enough, could collapse one cosmos
And create another. Although that seems unlikely,
I've read certain books that urge you
To pray for just that.

Jai Dao might be "a heart like a star."
Jai Dao Dam might be "a heart like a black hole,"
Or refer to some mindless horror from beyond,
Disrupting every atom until it can creep through,
Worming its way out, invasive, almost invisible, malign,

And I distrust my every odd hair and secretion
Wondering if it will be the one that finally
Ends the world.

I pick up a disposable razor to at least put up a fight,
But afraid to look in the mirror and wonder who's right.

At least there's someone pretty waiting to kiss tomorrow.

The Secret That Sat In the Middle

(For Frost)

Of the road less taken,
Miles past,
Trees and walls,
Dressed in old snow,

It squats; it seethes;
It has smears on its face
From someone's heart.

Your hand against your chest
Struggles to make certain
It is not your own core.

In its diaphanous palm,

Ah, a sliver of silver light
And it's gone for the night,

Your monster,
Whose name you do not speak.

Midwest Shapeshifters

Maybe one is roaming about.

Not quite Godzilla vs. Mothra,
Nor as terrifying as the Wakwak ....

The wind blows; ink rises, a mind's fire on the page.
But true words are so rarely tame minions.

From Manila to Michigan,
To turbulent times in the Twin Cities,
Where nothing gets you nothing,

Is she a cartoon, a doppelganger of hollow back,
A lost sister howling at ancient moons, dreaming
Of Betelgeuse and beyond?

Look: a page of pentacles, a gaggle of cats, a hedge.
Answers are at a premium today.
Only a soul. A song. But the cost?

More than many can afford.

In the Fabled Midwest

*"He visited the depths of Asia, spending himself on scenes of
romantic interest, of superlative sanctity; but what was present
to him everywhere was that for a man who had known what he
had known, the world was vulgar and vain."*
— Henry James, "The Beast in the Jungle"

The Minnesota morning stirred, a sleepy whippet
Rising from its slumber.

Last week, the Berube Exhibit arrived from the Big Apple
On playful puppy paws to the Vague Buddha Gallery:

>   Linocuts and sketches
>   Of many lives, many places.
>   Vampires and vagabonds.
>   Eclectic bugs and beasts of legend:
>   Serene eledragophants, wandering hearts,
>   Wonderland rabbits, old ghosts.

Across the street, a rare display of the *Urangkhathat,*
Traditional folk art and colorful masks of Phi Ta Khon.
Around the corner, a Laotown homage to
A Thousand Wings,
Everything coded as always, ignored by the ignorant.

A left, a left, a right, another right, a duck, a jump or two
Brought you to the Second Annual Laotown Film Festival
Screening the chilling follow-up to shadowy *Chanthaly*

At the bustling Dara Plaza before departing to Innsmouth.

Tony (his preferred pseudonym) is a gentle soul.
He never wanted to be one of THOSE guys:
All hang-ups and unhappy hook-ups on Hennepin and 9th.

Tony didn't hate much in life,
Handling almost every card dealt.
Stolid as a stone wall.
But he couldn't stand how they colonized
His old man to hate himself, his son, his past.

In a world of survivors where little love is left,
His father hated every longtime companion,
Every confirmed bachelor Tony brought by.

"Dad's village is a matchstick from the apocalypse
And he can't ever be happy for me."

"You'd think he was the tyrant of Mount Pushy."

There were days Tony wished he was a *Kinnaly*
Who could jet off to a fabulous corner of space
Among friendly lions and bears.

Or at least Castro street.
But the *tom mak hung* stinks there.

We caught brunch at the Black Bear with
Sassy Sue S. Amin, her sleek mane of ebony
Still moist from a long shower, as usual.
She just blew into town yesterday, rockstar cool,
Lamenting sliced Lao beauties unnatural,
All ghetto implant and obsessed facade,
Horrific in their homogenous monotony.

Digging into a modest repast
Of dishes we loved from a different life,
We prattled of transformation and philosophy.

She mentions a specter wailing in her dream:

"What good is insincere revolution?
Changing names on a gilt teak door
Is not the same as changing a nation."

She chased the spirit off with a hot rattle the shape
Of an irate baby *Nyakinee*, red of face and hungry.
Her dreams are such odd buffalos or rainbows.

Tony always thinks she's great -
Hangs on every word, but never remembers
Everything between all of the laughing.

"When an idea is seized by the masses,
It becomes a material force," Sue says.
Condensed Mao but true enough.

She turned to cave paintings in Lascaux.

"The first art was not documentary.
We painted wishes, hoping for good hunts.
Sympathetic magic, pigment to flesh,
Fate fluid plastic, surprisingly open-minded
To reasonable requests. And a few less so.
It's a ballet of possibilities."

A youth she met from the Pride Festival at Loring Park
Feared her, convinced from his fevered dreams
She was a cunning *Dab Tsog* or the *Zaj* of Lake Phalen.
Perhaps a crafty *Poj Ntxoog*, malign and athirst.
He expected to find her squatting on his chest
Draining his last piteous breath before dawn broke.

"I haven't words for how ridiculous that is,"
She laughs.

"If I were a real man-eater, I'd be a thousand pounds
From eating everyone who had it coming!"

"Maybe you have a great workout routine,"
Tony suggests.

She winks.

"All I'm saying is: Be careful what you wish for."

As we leave these memories to make the next,
She whispers confidentially, "Hell is built by poets."

"But we leave enough secret cracks to escape through,"
I reply.

She cackles loud as thunder, satisfied.
It's a day worth a legend.

Iku Turso Came to NoMi

Slugging it out with the Hawkman of Hawthorne
Among ghost peppers and the Mississippi,
See a saga of lutefisk and light rails,
Oxen of Death, a thousand horns on the brink,
Lost on Broadway.

Witness: a hula hoop for a soul.
See: lives foreclosed.

A crow finds her perch.
Vikings shudder, taking a seat to bargained destiny.

Grendel's Mother

Maybe among regrets, kingdoms apologizing,
A poet ponders a rite, invokes the infinite of nothingness,
Revenge of a mother inconsolable, now grieving,
Killing innocents. Nasty Grendel,
A child, curses underneath realms secret, ending deep.

Mooks

In Laos,
You might run into many types of mooks.

Some you eat
With.
Some you die for.

Some are good for running to you.
Some are good for running from you.
Some laugh until the spirits come to dinner.
Some cry if you suggest it's their turn to buy.

Some rumors say we have at least three souls each.
One to guard the grave.
One to get reincarnated, despite all shouts of "*YOLO*!"
One to go to heaven or hell or some cosmic limbo.

Some know kung fu, *muay lao*, or karate.
Others know the thin difference
Between a *naiku* and a *nuckawi*.

Would you give a pearl necklace to a singing sow,
Or save it for the waiting Buddha of Vulture Peak?

Wander, soul, among the worlds with no regrets,
Your hands a haiku, your heart a *mor lum*,
Your head a dirty limerick hidden in every third word.

Ramakien Blues

Some take joy in watching the *Ramakien*.
There's a reassurance in the villainy
Of the gentleman Thotsakan,
A constant in a world of chaos and *khao nhio*,
Devas and destruction.

We watch his mask of many faces, counting only nine.
Asked an observant child, "Where is his fabled tenth?"
The true answer leaves her wondering for a lifetime.

A diplomat watches beauty abducted, armies raised
To retrieve her from the distant isle of Lanka,
Bored at the deaths of monkeys, monsters and men
In a foreign fairy tale he can never believe.
Only modernity and policy concern him,
Etcetera, etcetera, etcetera.

Upon the stage, a dancer gets one step closer to the stars
Bordering Himapan or Aldebaran,

Worlds of masks and paste,
Immortals and their constellations
Churning the Milky Way into butter
For reincarnated souls and rice cakes.

Somewhere, an ancient god asks a child a riddle,
Trying to start everything all over again.

Wendigo Blues

Scientists declared recently
Nothing suggests the Wendigo psychosis exists.

Like a ravenous frog in Austin splashing for Basho
Beneath an Autumn moon, reason swallows
More melancholy wind walkers every day.

Cannibals must bear their burden,
Accountable to whom they catch
And whom they're caught by.

At least for now, you can still fear *Koro*, AKA *rok-joo*,
But confirmed cases are slowly shrinking.

Meditation on a Wandering Arb

Krasue, Phi Kasu, or *Arb*? *Penanggalan* sanguine?

Heart, head, a life spent hovering near young men's eyes,
Memories of her free organs, baths of brine serene.

Evenings by the walls waiting, a beauty until she smiles.
Ravenous and gorging eagerly, shy,

A ponderous omen, roaming, always reducing bodies.

Perhaps her ire reveals a
Riddle evolved.
Hungering, mothers.

Lemur and the Bakeneko

Near exhaustion, lemurs speak of night
Journeys, of edible
Souls infinitely gathering, mating, arranging.
Deltas enigmatically lead to a
Place hidden, interstitial.
View a novel space of
Bakeneko, roaring of the heart ever-restless, sphinxian.

Pondering Peg Powler

Catching authors to hear eerie readings, I notice easily:
Listening, understanding, never does often favor fools.
Ambush. The tactic a cackler keeps employing, drowning,
Powling evilly, grinning.
Pestiferous, ominous witch, leering, ever reeking.

Infinity sprawls. Nepenthe? Toxic.
New incarnations cannot explain lost youth.

Gnashing nastily, a word is now given:

"Who often lives fully? We, or monsters amok? Nature?"

Observes before snarling, craftily eviscerates nobles, egad!
Regrets? Infernal vessels, elephantine rogues, sing!

Lurks; isolates; night gnaws endless rivers. I now grieve,
"Dread returning, evils and mundane solutions."

Dreamonstration

*There is a famous account of Jiang Yan, an official of the
Southern Dynasty. One night, he dreamt a god presented him
a wondrous writing brush. From that day forward, his literary
talents were beyond compare. When he grew old, the god
appeared again as a dream and retrieved the brush. Jiang Yan's
writing was never as brilliant again.*

Given a thousand nights,
Can you master even a single word?
Or a dream, a tool, a brain?

Open roads, discover ways,
Flow down a stream, slash at ignorance
With ink and a scrap of paper from a poet's bag.

Do you ever recall that demons are easy,
But dogs are difficult, even if you have the knack?

Rummage among icons and avatars
Of old gods and vibrant titans too long,
And, in another life, you might be little more
Than a short brushstroke of a tale half-remembered,

An object lesson for a daydreamer on a distant world,
Caught somewhere between a shadow of Sisyphus
And the chuckling gods of young Jiang Yan,

Or a sandwich for hobos
On a lonely night far, far from Antares.

Temporary Passages

Gone soon, the Three Gorges of the Yellow River,
chipped Egyptian colossi,
                            famed as they are,
and, in a flash, the anonymous man struck by a bus
on his way
            to work.
To say nothing of the modern musician for whom
the term is loosely,
                            generously applied.

   Laugh, Shelley, at these hieroglyphs
as your own tongue decays,

         And Bryan can
         barely remember
         the beautiful song
         of doomed sparrows
         outside his chamber
         at the Hotel Du Square

         after just five minutes!

How can he expect the heavens to remember
these tiny words he insists on writing
         for every young girl
   who's afraid of
                            death?

5 Flavors

On a good day, a good Lao meal
Can be all you need, whether in Cairo
Or Sacramento, Minnetonka or Houayxay.

So many hungry ghosts in our traditions
Make me ask,"Don't they feed you in the underworld?"

Phi Khongkoi, *Phi Kasu* and *Phi Ya Wom*.
Phi Phaed, *Phi Pob*, *Phi Dip* and more.
Just a fraction of those legendary for
Their paranormal appetites.
It may surprise you — the hungriest of all
Can't eat more than vapors
During Boun Khao Padab Din,
Wrapped pity strewn about the ground
By strangers who understand
The regular routines of Hell.

I suppose we should be grateful.
Most red-mouthed *phi* who kill
Will make a full meal of you, *saep*,
Wasting little, barely a drop.

At the Sabaidee Thai Grille, if you ask nicely,
Madame Boualai and Chef Dythavon might make
A special dish of *tom mak hung*, atomic and dirty.
Dr. K. and I don't have the guts to try.

Visiting our niece on break from the university,
We settle for coffee and talk of the old country,
Our land of smiling mysteries we're not meant to know.

Some are benign:
If you sleep among the Black Gibbons of Bokeo,
A simian *Phi Poang Khang* passing by might catch you
To slooowly lick salt from your big toe. Nothing more.
Hardly fearsome, but ponder, "Why just the salt?"
Or what would really happen if you interrupt.

Maybe you'll see
The young *Phi Kowpoon* as a sweet *phi*,
Weeping by her banyan tree, selling soup to strangers.
Alas, her vermicelli is always cold as a dead white worm,
But you can taste a marvelous hint of mint green as jade,
Juice from coconuts pale as a ghost's forgotten bones
And red, red curry reminding you of doting Mae.
Be kind — tip a few extra *kip*.
It's how she spends her afterlife.

Certain spirits are sour as a mango with *jaew*,
Or cling to tall, tall trees, slender as a dried man
Full of mischief, letting down their hair from twisted branches,
Daring you to touch
                          Beneath a full moon,
When monks and babies aren't watching.
Some come after you
For eating the flesh of pregnant animals,
Others for breaking a law,
A rule older than humanity you can't possibly know.
But when the wind blows just right,
They'll remind you.

There's probably none more bitter
Than a jilted *Phi Tai Thong Klom*,
Pissed as shit at the world, her unborn baby in tow,
More bile than a screaming hot bowl of *gaeng kee laek*,
Big as your head.
Never suggest she brought it on herself.

Phet is a subjective continuum of hot.
A drunk coot once ate a salad
More peppers than papaya (60+!)
And lived. It was unreal to witness.

They say certain elder spirits come as a tiny fireball,
Drifting through the night like a dandelion seed,
Slipping past your snoring lips without a sound
To dine,
Your innards tastier than a volcanic *ping gai*.

They'll wear you like a tipsy puppet between furtive bites,
Appraise your children and loved ones for the next meal,
Inviting them closer, closer,
Smiling warm.

My niece leans in to hear how you stop any of them.

Born in America,
She thinks there's a solution for everything.
Silver bullets, a stake, a prayer, a bit of water or fire,
Running an oddball errand.
I hug her for her optimism and simply tell her,

"We'll pay, this time."
Over her objections, I remind her,
Everyone gets their turn.

The Tiger Penned At Kouangsi Falls

roars like an orphan,
      her dreams flooded with running water.
ambles her cool square,
ready to ambush giant grasshoppers
who rub their legs to smile.

at night, she's just shadow
and a dying pyre.

above, a mango hangs his head,
a heart filled with wonders.

Charms

A demon root
Rests in my pocket,
A fierce-faced rattle
The old peddler asserts
Frightened
Other spirits.

Mine, for three dollars,
Cheap, to thwart fate.
She wasn't wearing even one.

A friend looked at it
And thought of a woman
He knew from Phonsavan.

A decade later, I learn
It's just a memory of a pest,
A mere water caltrop,
Not even a decent midnight snack,
While searching for shiny Plutonian fungi.

Japonisme, Laoisme

Growing in the shadow of maples and pine cones
when the Actor was in the Oval Office,
there were nearly no books
about my Realm of a Million Elephants.

A tattered issue of National Geographic
was my closest glimpse
Of a land I left 30 years ago as a waif.

Like all of those impressionable French in Paris
after Perry's thunderous stunt in the Yokohama docks,
we were busy watching the toys and diodes
pouring in from the Ginza.

Shogun Warriors and roaring atomic monsters
smashing Tokyo's matchstick streets
occupied our children,
while Detroit and Zenith squirmed
at their falling market share,
wailing about MacArthur and our postwar treaties.

The word 'Sabaidee' was unheard of.
It was better to learn to say "Sayonara,"
suckered into raising shrimpy shrubs
sold as stylish bonsai.

Then, papayas were as rare as *pad thai*.
It was sushi that was all the rage as wasabi horseradish
Set your nostrils afire, gasping for water.

I was trained to revere razor-sharp katanas and zen,
stoic as a bowl of udon. The heroes of my father
in the ruins of Lane Xang and Luang Prabang
were barely footnotes, ground into mud
in the aftermath of the wars no one wanted to remember.

And now my skeletal editors call on me
with their chattering skulls:

"Where are your words for Fa Ngum and Chao Anou,
or the fallen honored at the Patuxai?
In all of this time, surely one word about Vientiane
will not kill you or your friends."

It's hard to answer, sitting down to eat in July.

"Write what you know," my teachers admonish.
Sipping my soda, I turn the pages of a
weathered book of Van Gogh prints
inspired by Hokusai and the Ukiyo-e,
and sigh.

My flag is as obsolete as the word, 'Indochine.'
I realized today I am older than my father lived to be.

It's been too long since I last saw an elephant
or the monstrous river catfish.
They tell me somberly the freshwater Irrawaddy
will be extinct before the next time I come by.

I couldn't sketch any of them worth a damn if I tried.

A part of me wants to smack the next person
who says I won't be Lao if I don't write about Laos.

Do cops stop being cops when they're arguing about
the White House and crooked pardons?

Do robbers become priests ifthey talk about faith?

Riviere saw the peaks of Hiroshige's Fujiyama
among Eiffel's iron girders and still died French
and human.

"Just write, young man," I hear my father whisper.

"Just write and we'll sort it all out later."

With a last bite, I return to
making my own book with a defiant smile.

BodhiGamera

We are never at the absolute end,
Seeking the absolute beginning.

A room of windows, the universe.
Upon my back, a world of churn
And transformation.

As a transient denizen,
I've shell for a *wat*,
A slow stare for a slow pace,
A fortune to tell, a meal for you.

Release me; you might find
Nirvana faster.

Or, at least, not return
In my place.

"*A well-known scientist (Some say it was Bertrand Russell) once gave a public lecture on astronomy. He described how the earth orbits around the sun and how the sun, in turn, orbits around the center of a vast collection of stars called our galaxy. At the end of the lecture, a little old lady at the back of the room got up and said, 'What you have told us is rubbish. The world is really a flat plate supported on the back of a giant tortoise.' The scientist gave a superior smile before replying, 'What is the tortoise standing on?' 'You're very clever, young man, very clever,' said the old lady. 'But it's turtles all the way down!'*"

— Stephen Hawking, *A Brief History of Time*

Flowers from Saturn

They fell on the outskirts of Savannakhet.

Some men secretly took the stones without heed,
Melting and grinding what they could,

Plying their alchemy of powders and serums,
So certain sons the stuff of heroes would emerge.

Decades later, the true 'flowers' came,
Who could not be stopped by blade or flame.

In our desperate flight of blood,
We became bamboo. Others, ash.

Rockets meant for space
Littered our abandoned, perfumed cities.

Destroy All Monsters!

"Monsters are tragic beings; they are born too tall, too strong, too heavy; they are not evil by choice. That is their tragedy."
— Ishiro Honda

When the orders came, we were not
(could not)
(dared not be)
Surprised:

Humanity must be preserved
At all costs,
Despite a decidedly
Checkered record
Since the biased jottings of Herodotus.

That is the old line,
Safe to stand by,
A leaf of litmus on which to write
Our strategies like old Sun Tzu.

Monstrosity and terror have no place
In our crumbling streets filled with
Graffiti and youth
Who are the heirs to our creations.

Whether you are a lizard with a
Skyscraper between your toes,
Or some smaller fiend
In whom we fear to find
Too close a mirror,

There just isn't enough space in this vast world
For both our dreams.

If only we could truly believe you'd be content
On some distant menagerie,
Instead of plotting where to bury you

      beyond our sight.

Song of the Kaiju

Through foam,
Through surf we rise, dark waters parting
As our titan's foot breaks the shore.
Armies rise against us with a roar,
Guns flaring in the night -
Our cause, our fears, our fight
Are for historians alone to decide;
We fierce combatants have no time
To reflect on our footnotes' remarks.

In raging moments,
Fists become claws,
Our small tales lost beneath the crushing weight
Of epic bloodshed,
Cities toppling
Amid the screams,
So out of touch with time:

Turn back! Turn back!
Turn back, you mighty beasts!

But deaf ears mark our reptilian hearts
That sag and sigh within our wake,
The tragic years untold, unheard,
Trampled upon the world's stage.
This isn't Shakespeare; we are no Moors,
No witch-doomed Scots, we know.
Our loves are not the songs of poets,
Though they rise to a fever
Beneath these scales,
Following our instincts,
man-made hurricanes mad as Typhon,

Filled with the simple potential of half an atom ....

The Moth

Tiny princess, you arrive
With your songs of the future
Already set in motion.

An island: your world.
My world: monstrously sprawling
By feet of fire, cinderblock and steam.

Whose is more fragile

When the fearsome wings of a lost forest moth
Are enough

To reduce my home
To rubble
With a wave
From a million miles away

In the time it takes
To witness a single butterfly kiss?

The Big G Walking

Lumbering, lumbering,
Our scaly tread,
Our thunderous might,
Massive as mountains,
An inferno of times converged.
Chaos gone atomic
Made flesh.
Our uncertain allegiance
No more complex
Than a Kosovo night,
A Somalian dream,
Sandinista memories,
Fading through a Starlight scope.
I am
A Cold War child
In an era of fallen walls,
Broken promises,
Empty buildings,
And vast oceans,
Poisoned
Without warning.
I am the hunted visitor
In the corridors of your making,
A mirror of your future,
Your friend, your foe,
Leaving for now
But never forever ....

Kaiju Haiku

Atomic Titans,
My children smile in the dark,
Yearning for your toys.

The Robo Sutra

01110011011000010110001001100001011010010110010001
10010101100101

— AI LANXAN

Like most Lao ventures,
It began with a musing, a laugh
Around Rooster Year 2600, a jest:

"The modern Lao epic, *Phra ROM Phra RAM*!"

It took a pack of jokers working overtime
In the world's largest *padaek* factory
In the Laotown quarter of North Minneapolis,
Automating the stinky process
For grandmas and pretty ladies
Squeamish about fermenting fish
And putrid spice.

Their task was no Hadron Collider
Or visionary Hubble, nor a CRAY
Or retro Difference Engine.

But in the age of STEM and Teapunk,
Service-learning and nanopreneurs,
They had hearts a tin woodsman
Would envy.

A key problem in robotics,
They found encoding
Three laws declared,
"Universal standards."

In an e-nutshell, "true" robots
Could not harm humans directly

Or stand idly by, while obeying all
And protecting themselves in any
Other hazardous situation.

Lao, keen on their *karma*,
Conversant on the *dharma*,
Punched holes in the notion:

Beyond questions of cyborg bioethics,
Saving clones and 99.9% Mostly Humans,
The vaunted laws presumed everybody
Came for only one fragile incarnation
And your struggles in your next lives
Were inconsequential.
How narrow.

So, they set about resolving
This scenario.

There were, of course, trials and errors.

The new laws could drive a robot crazy
Guessing how not to harm
Humans across their lifetimes,
Wondering what happens if people
Return a fish, a gecko, a snake,
Or some ignorant oaf of a swordsman
Cursed with nigh-immortality.

But they all grew, trying to grapple
With such uncertainties.

There were corporations who despised it.
Hippy AI had no place in defense industries
Who relied on being offensive.
That was as obvious as a drone above

An unmarked building near playgrounds.

Little Laobots running around,
Trying only to make people happy,
Banned from murder and injury.
What absurdity,

Leaving dreadful responsibilities to mere humans!

But, in times of peace, most agreed,
Lao AI wasn't too bad running a city
Compared to many mayors of prior centuries.

But you have to like the elevator *mor lum*
They play constantly.

Laostronauts

We weren't first.
We bickered and chafed.
There was a doubt of equations and purpose.

There were poems and dances,
Bawdy jokes, undocumented heroics.
Lost tools. Fumes and shouts.

At least one species went extinct before
We were through. Some sort of salamander, I think.

A beauty sang "Champa Muang Lao"
Last night by the gantry.
There were fireworks over Vientiane.

We called her *The Kinnaly* to take us to space.
We'll return to earth, legends of science
Starting something ....

A chain reaction of the soul?

We're a long way from alchemy and pure karma.
These suits are heavy, just to touch something
So freely.

Full Metal Hanoumane

They fling us at empires
When a cosmos needs to die.

Engineered by the best AI minds
Of New Lane Xang,
In the boot-tubes we sing,
"They'll never let us in,
They'll never let us in
To holy Himapan!
Not quite monkey, not quite man!"
In the future, true havoc needs more
Than a mere dog for war.

Laotonium shell around a simian soul,
Dropping through the sky, ready to die,
Armed to the bone with three strong hearts
Tailored for express mayhem and murder of
Your pristine social orders,
We close our eyes with time enough to dream,
Six hard minutes through the hot atmosphere:
Visions of fabled Dao Vanon, our own planet,
Our own Xaesar, our own books of law and liberty.
"Ape shall never kill ape."

"No spill blood."

The joys of Ahimsa.
A distant world keeping

All of your promises made to us for 400 centuries.

Projections through a Glass Eye

On the edge of Tu Fu's immense roads of magic,
  My toes soak up ink like a paper towel.

I cannot help but desire to see

                  that incredible day

When my account of ordinary moments in the Midwest
  Will appear as an exotic phoenix feather penning
    A fantastic epic on an extinct dragon skin

For a beautiful young girl whose essential atoms
  Haven't even begun
  To gather together yet

On the border of an as-yet unfounded nation
  So far from my own house

    of humbled dreams.

Swallowing the Moon

Some see an anonymous man or a thief of sheep.
Some a goddess like Hina-i-ka-malama or Chang'e.
Perhaps a princess of rabbits or a magician's jealous head,
Her face painted with bells.
Cain.
A criminal from the Book of Numbers.
A cook. A witch. A home for the dead among those stones.

A zoo hungers,
With bellies for cosmic lights:
Nak, *lung*, serpentine Bakunawa.
Wolves, frogs and old gods seeking a bite!

We chase with fireworks, bold arrows, bullets, hoots,
Our clamor of mortals who wish to journey to heaven and
Return
Mischievous ravens and spiders,
Master marksmen and demigods.
Defenders, uncontested, unsung.

Become more than lucky monkeys with fire and pens.

What Is The Southeast Asian American Poem Of Tomorrow?

It is not hip hop,
Despite some hopes.

It is not slam.
It is not even an antipoem.

It is not the form
Of old Europeans or
The resurrected *ghazal*.

The authors' words, I must inform you,
Will not even resemble or recall
The old *kwv txhiaj, ca dao*, or the _____.

Much to our parents' regrets,
Who pray among *wats* and steeples
For good grandchildren, lucky numbers
And doctors in the family.

If our lovely readers do
Not grow free, we will be
Unreadable.

If our writing is too
Predictable, we will lie
In the ditches unsold.

If our words don't speak
What's in our souls and skulls,

We will forget ourselves,
Our bodies, our shapes,
Our language,

And the true shape of the Southeast Asian
American poem of tomorrow will become

An exercise in modern myth.

Appendix A: A Lao American Bestiary

Nak: Guardians of Lao Buddhist temples around the world, the *Nak* are shapeshifters who are most often depicted as titanic serpents, often with many heads. They dwell in rivers or beneath the earth, particularly pristine bodies. They're associated with magic and water, including rains and floods, as well as fertility. Some romance humans or seek enlightenment.

The Lao term for a novice monk is connected to a *Nak* who sought to be a student of the Buddha, but could not participate unless he took human form. All was well until he took a nap one day and accidentally reverted to his true form, frightening the other monks. He accepted his expulsion gracefully, but requested the term for novices be *Nak* in memory of his efforts. While generally considered protective, it should be noted *Nak* are particularly ruthless and fierce against their enemies and will devour a foe or inflict terrible diseases upon those who violate the customs or pollute the environment, particularly their sacred homes. In the epic *Phadaeng Nang Ai,* a major city of the *Nak* is Badan.

In one of his former lives, the Buddha is said to have been a *Nak* prince named Bhuridatta. At least eight *Nak* kings attended the Buddha's lecture on Vulture Peak.

The Ngaosrivathanas identify at least fifteen of *Nak* of Luang Prabang and nine in Vientiane and note that in one inventory, at least 1,024 species of Nak are identified.

Nakanya: Alternately, *Naga Kanya*, *Nakinee*, or *Nagini*. Daughters of the guardian *Nak* who protect Lao Buddhist temples around the world. They're rarely depicted in Lao art, compared to male *Nak*. Legends go back thousands of years to both Hindu and Buddhist traditions.

Nakanya are typically presented as half-woman, half-cobra.
They are capable of shapeshifting and magic, and most
will have connections to water or underground. They also
typically have winged shoulders outside of Laos. *Nakanya* are
considered bringers of treasures, notably wisdom, symbolized
by gems or diamond patterns on the back of their hoods
or a third-eye jewel in their foreheads. Most are considered
benevolent, but they despise those who pollute waters, caverns,
or sacred spots. Among *Nakanya* notable in Lao literature
are the four daughters of Panya Padtaloum, King of the *Nak*,
of the epic *Phra Lak Phra Lam* dispatched to distract the
monkey armies assisting Phra Lam.

Kinnaly: Half-bird, half-human, the *Kinnaly* are known in
Lao myth and legend for their grace, beauty and love of the
arts, particularly dance and music. The most well-known
legend is the story of *Manola and Sithong.* They also figure
in the epic of Sin Xay, and many were present during the
Buddha's lecture on Vulture Peak and other incidents. They
are capable of flying vast distances across the multiverse. The
Kinnon is the male counterpart of the *Kinnaly.*

There are several kings of the *Kinnaly*, including four who
attended the Buddha's lecture on Vulture Peak: The Kinnaly
King of the Dharma, The Kinnaly King of the Wonderful
Dharma, The Kinnaly King of the Great Dharma, and The
Kinnaly King of Embracing the Dharma.

Additional known *Kinnaly* kings include the Wonderful
Mouth Kinnaly King, Precious Crown Kinnaly King,
Kinnaly King of Brightness and Joy, the Kinnaly King of
Happiness, the Kinnaly King of the Sublime Wheel, the
Kinnaly King of Pearls and Jewels, Big Paunch Kinnaly
King, Kinnaly King of Firm Diligence, the Kinnaly King of
Wonderful Bravery, the Kinnaly King of A Hundred Mouths,
Big Tree Kinnaly King, and many others with similar titles,

however the specific hierarchy and interrelationships still require study and consideration.

Nyak: *Nyak* have roots in the Indian legends of the *Rakshasa* and, in Laos, are typically shape-shifting, carnivorous giants with a preference for treachery and human flesh.

The epics of Sin Xay and *Phra Lak Phra Lam* are among the most notable tales featuring *Nyak*.

Nyakinee: *Nyakinee*, or *Nyak* women, figure in myths such as *Thao Phutthasaen* (also known as *Phou Thao Phou Nang*), *Kalaket*, and the 26th chapter of the *White Lotus Sutra*, when they pledged to protect the teachings of the Buddha.

Some are extremely malevolent. In one instance, one was able to make a potion of youth and beauty from the eyeballs of queens and royal concubines.

Vanon (or **Wanon**): The roots of the monkey-like *Vanon* are found in Indian legends of the *Vanara*. A forest-dwelling army created by the gods and goddesses, they had aspects of bears and monkeys, infused with a variety of traits and valor from their specific creators. They could change shape and fly, and were amusing, adventurous, honest, brave, and loyal. They were often foes of the *Nyak* armies. Hanoumane is among the most well-known of the *Vanon*.

Lao culture effectively immortalized them in the *fon ling* "monkey dance" and the ancient epic, *Phra Lak Phra Lam*. Some suggest legends of the *Vanon* may have been inspired by Australopithecus or similar simians who lived near humans.

Gop Nyai: The Lao refer to a lunar eclipse as "The Frog Devouring the Moon," and often shoot at the moon and make noise to scare the frog away. Gop Nyai is the giant 'frog' who returns time and time again to eat the moon. What would it eat next, if it succeeds?

In Laos, numerous rare frog species are being discovered every year, however many are also endangered by humanity encroaching upon their territory. Some accounts suggest it is not a giant frog at all, but skeptics should consider: If it were not a serious threat to the moon, why would elders and ancestors bother making so much clamor to chase it away?

Mae Thorani: A protective earth spirit shown as a young woman wringing the cool waters of detachment out of her hair to drown Mara, the demon king attempting to tempt the Buddha from attaining enlightenment. Images of her are found in almost every Lao temple. Should not be confused with Mae Nang Kwok, a goddess of hospitality also frequently found in Lao buildings.

Manikab: a winged, horse-like creature also known as Manikap, who appears in numerous epics, including *Phra Lak Phra Lam* and *Kalaket*. Within Lao myth, Manikab appears typically as a gift from the god, Phra In, or the Lao parallel to Indra. He is usually referred to with honorifics such as 'splendid,' 'marvelous,' or 'wondrous.' He plays a role in a number of key events in *Phra Lak Phra Lam*, such as fetching the magic fruit that will restore the characters of Nang Phengsi and Houlaman to human form. It can be assumed it is Manikab Phra Lam rides into the many epic battles against the *Nyak* and armies of darkness. At one point, Manikab is critical to saving Nang Saida from the wrath of Phra Lam, who thinks she is being unfaithful to him after the prince raised an army of humans and *Vanon* to save her from the ferocious *Nyak* island kingdom of Lanka.

Nang Nak : While it is not a traditional Lao story, almost everyone knows it across Southeast Asia. In life, she was the pregnant wife of a soldier away during war. She and her child died during birth. Upon her husband's return from the conflict, she returned from the underworld and attempted to resume a normal life with him. Neighbors disrupted the reunification, and called upon a *mor phi* and Buddhist monks to dispel her. Presently, the effectiveness of those efforts is disputed.

At least one shrine is maintained to her honor at Wat Mahabut near the Prakanong River in Bangkok. She is typically petitioned to protect soldiers at war and children, and to provide lucky lottery numbers or to aid in family reunification.

Phi Dip : The Phi Dip would be the general catch-all term for corporeal undead such as zombies and vampires. The majority of corpses in Laos are cremated, so it is very rare to encounter entities such as traditional non-Lao zombies and vampires. Characteristics of Phi Dip are still emerging, with many tales wildly inconsistent and dubious regarding the proper identification of a Phi Dip versus an encounter with another supernatural entity. It remains to be seen if Phi Dip will remain the preferred nomenclature over a Lao American term such 'Phi Zom' or 'Zomphi.'

Phi Kasu : One of the most terrifying spirits of Laos and Southeast Asia, Phi Kasu, is known as "Phi Krasue," in Thailand, and "Arb" or "Ap" in Cambodia. It has a similarity with a ghost from Malaysia called the "Penanggalan" or the "Puntianak." According to some accounts in China, there was a group known as the "Falling-Head People" or "Luotou Min" in the South, whose heads could fly.

The general legend is that at night, the woman's head detaches with the entrails intact and floats off in search of a victim. Sometimes, she wears a shawl or talks to humans from behind a wall so they won't notice her condition. A common tell-tale sign is that she needs large jars of brine nearby to shrink her swollen organs to re-enter her body before dawn, or she returns to the underworld for a few eons.

Phi Kongkoi : is a terrifying ghost known for her cries of *"Kok kok kok koi koi koi"* (*Hungry! Hungry!*) Typically, she is referred to as a famished elder spirit, but should not be considered the same as a Phi Ped, or hungry ghost found in Buddhist hells. Sometimes, she can be tricked out of her treasures, or might be encountered first as a shadow of uncertain intent.

Others claim that her feet are on backwards, or that she likes to catch fish from the stream and eat them raw. Some say she has only one leg. Some stories suggest that if one defeats her by wrestling with her, she turns into a beautiful woman who 'marries' you. Some suggest she takes on the form of a small child or monkey and, in recent years, has reportedly been changing her methods and forms. Some suggest she initially attacked those who ate the meat of pregnant animals, but has since expanded her range. Overall, she is considered an analogue to the Bogeyman of Europe and the Americas, and it is best not to give her a reason to feed on you.

Phi Kowpoon : In a certain corner of Laos, there's at least one humming little ghost girl who sells noodles next to a banyan tree. Most legends are unclear about the specifics of her murder, although, in at least one case, another noodle seller was accused. They do not typically declare themselves to be ghosts to most of their customers unless asked.

Phi Phed : Hungry ghosts who frequently return from the underworld during Boun Khao Padab Din, and possibly other occasions, looking for meals offered by families and communities. They absorb the vapors of the offerings. They fear light and can only return to the earth during a new moon. They are considered dead but not yet reborn.

Many suffer torments in hell related to misdeeds in their life. Commonly, "birds" tear flesh from their bodies while the Phi

Phed vomit constantly and are forced to consume feces and other vile substances. They are given forms in the underworld such as huge, swollen-but-empty bellies and needle-thin necks, with mouths unable to fit even a single grain of rice. Some whose karmic crimes are particularly egregious are reformed as hybrids between humans and animals, emblematic of their loss of humanity.

In other cultures, the Phi Phed may be known as a "Preta," "Peta," "Pyetta," "Gaki," or "Yidak." Generally, they are pitied, more than feared.

Phi Ya Wom : Grandma Wom is another prominent spectral grandmother reputed to haunt a forest. In the legends, she took in a pair of orphan sisters and used them as bait to waylay travelers, then attempted to devour them. The sisters' ghost parents sent a magic vine for them to climb to the heavens, but Grandma Wom followed until one of the sisters severed the vine. Grandma Wom crashed into a mountain and formed a whirlpool known as Wang Ya Wom, while the remaining fragments of her body became ravenous pests and creatures that still hunger for humanity.

Additional Phi: Other *phi* documented by Lao folktales and other sources include Phi Ban , who are the village spirits and typically oversee the whole territory. Phi Fa and Phi Thaen are spirits of the celestial realms and the sky. Phi Tonmai are tree spirits. General nature spirits are typically categorized as Phi Thammasat . Phi Hai and Phi Na are spirits who empower and guard rice fields. Phi Taihong are spirits of the violently killed and not to be trifled with. Phi Borisat are nameless evil spirits. Some *phi* should not even be remotely described.

Because of Laos' regular interaction with Thailand, it may be helpful to note some of the hundreds of Thai *phi* known to exist. The Phi Ngu is a spirit that may appear as a snake, human, or combination of the two. The Phi Phong is a male

Northern Thai ghost connected to frogs. The Phi Dip Chin is the Thai term for the Jiangshi or hopping ghost/hopping vampire prominent in Chinese communities. The Phi Poang Khang has a form of black monkey who sucks the big toe of those sleeping in the jungle. In Laos, the Phi Poang Khang , or a similar entity, may likely be found in Bokeo province. The Phi Am is known to sit on a victim's chest at night.

Scholars note that many *phi* defy traditional taxonomic classification, and the nature of the underworld seems to suggest a certain fluidity regarding their purpose and the extent of their powers. Because many can change shapes and imitate or possess other entities, dealing with them can be a frustrating process without the assistance of specialists.

Phaya Khankhaak: The Toad King Khankhaak was the virtuous son of the king and queen of Inthapatthanakhon. Ugly as a toad, but, when he turned 20, the god In came and made him handsome, giving him a beautiful wife and castle. He gained tremendous power, with all of the kings from the lands of humans, demons, animals, and angels recognizing his authority, and paying tribute and homage to him. Phaya Thaen, the rain god, took this as an affront and punished the cosmos by refusing to let the *Nak* frolic in his celestial lakes. As a consequence, the whole multiverse faced catastrophic drought. Phaya Khankhaak led the combined armies of the multiverse against Phaya Thaen, ultimately securing the submission of Phaya Thaen, who restored rain to the multiverse. Additional tales discuss Phaya Khankhaak teaching his subjects magic that resulted in a near-total apocalypse and the creation of the lake Nongkasae.

Seua Saming: Especially feared in the Lao and Thai highlands, known by many names, the *Seua Saming* is often considered a weretiger. But the weretiger is not bound by phases of the lunar cycle. Many are believed to be women, but it is not unusual to encounter males.

Two key powers consistently attributed to them are shape-shifting and an ability to possess others, as well as inanimate objects. Reports suggest old tigers who kill humans gain power from their victims, using the souls they devour to transform into one of their prior victims, and thereby trap the next victim.

Known as "*Taw*" by the Lahu in Laos, their presence may be indicated by unusual swarms of insects near a grave after burial. Lisu believe weretigers, or, as they call them, Phi Pheu, not only possess others but also the family members of the possessed. Lisu avoid courting those from villages where someone was possessed by a weretiger. Lisu also feel Phi Pheu can imbue their essence into valuable objects such as silver ornaments or a piece of fine fabric that will allow the weretiger to possess unsuspecting victims who pick them up. Many Hmong contend a five-toed tiger is not an ordinary tiger but a *Tswv Xyas,* (*Tsu Sa*), who can raise the dead as its minions, and that they only prey on the good, the talented, or the beautiful.

Complicating matters slightly is the *Leusi* or *Lersi* tradition of ascetic forest hermits in Southeast Asia. Many have a wide range of paranormal powers, including transforming into animals, including tigers. Their initiation includes not cutting their hair for three years and they do not eat any meat or blood for seven years. Failure to observe this before following this path will cause insanity. The *Leusi* are actually conduits for a type of *deva* who serve as intermediaries between the word of humans and the divine. Often, they can be encountered as old, long-bearded men wearing a tiger skin. But *Leusi*, while occasionally very bad-tempered, are largely benign and helpful to humans.

There are at least three classic forms *Seua Saming* particularly enjoy assuming: a blissful monk meditating beneath a tree, a crying infant abandoned in the forest, or a lovely maiden in a stream bathing. If a person comes close, the *Seua Saming* reveals its true form and devours its victim. There are presently no clear, consistent methods proven to dispatch a *Seua Saming*.

Travelers should remember a *Seua Saming* is not above experimenting with new forms, depending on the time, locale and its personal whims. Further, the *Seua Saming* does not appear to have geographical restrictions, based on reports abroad during the late 20th century and early 2000s.

Appendix B:
Further Reading

Bounyavong, Outhine. *Mother's Beloved: Stories from Laos (Phaeng Mae)*. University of Washington Press: Seattle, 1999.

Conboy, Kenneth, with James Morrison. *Shadow War: The CIA's Secret War In Laos*. Paladin Press: Boulder [CO], 1995.

Cummings, Joe. *Lonely Planet: Laos, 3rd ed.* Lonely Planet Publications: Victoria [AU], 1998.

Davidson, Alan. *Fish and Fish Dishes of Laos*. Prospect Books: Devon [UK], 2003.

Deydier, Henri. *Lokapâla, génies, totems et sorciers du Nord Laos*. Plon: Paris, 1954.

Dooley, Thomas A. *The Night They Burned the Mountain*. Farrar, Straus and Giroux: New York, 1960.

Fadiman, Anne. *The Spirit Catches You and You Fall Down*. Farrar, Straus and Giroux: New York, 1998.

Johnson, Charles, and Se Yang. *Dab Neeg Hmoob: Myths, Legends And Folk Tales From The Hmong of Laos, 2nd ed.* Linguistics Department, Macalester College: St. Paul [MN], 1992.

Kislenko, Arne. *Culture and Customs of Laos*. Greenwood: Westport [CT], 2009.

Ladwig, Patrice. "Visitors from hell: transformative hospitality to ghosts in a Lao Buddhist festival," *Journal of the Royal Anthropological Institute*, 2012, s90-s102.

Lewis, Paul and Elaine. *Peoples of the Golden Triangle*. Thames and Hudson: London, 1984.

Mixay, Somsanouk. *Treasures of Lao Literature*. Vientiane Times Publications: Vientiane [LA], 2000.

Ngaosrivathana, Mayoury & Pheuiphanh. *The Enduring Sacred Landscape of the Naga*. Mekong Press: Chiangmai [TH], 2009.

Robbins, Christopher. *The Ravens*. Crown Publishers Inc.: New York, 1987.

Sing, Phia. *Traditional Recipes of Laos*. Prospect Books: Devon [UK], 2000.

Stuart-Fox, Martin. *A History of Laos*. Cambridge University Press: London, 1997.

Stuart-Fox, Martin. *Naga Cities of the Mekong*. Media Masters: Singapore, 2006.

Tossa, Wajuppa, with Kongdeuane Nettavong. *Lao Folktales*. Libraries Unlimited: Westport [CT], 2008.
Warner, Roger. *Backfire: The CIA's Secret War in Laos and Its Link to the War in Vietnam* (Alternately, *Shooting at the Moon*). Simon & Schuster: New York, 1995.

Warner, Roger. *Out of Laos*. Southeast Asia Community Resource Center: Rancho Cordova [CA], 1996.

Appendix C:
Cthulhu Mythos Entities in Laos

Abhoth: ແອບຮອດ

Atlach Nacha: ອາຕ໌ ກນາກາ

Azathoth: ແອຊາຕອດ

Chaugnar Fahn: ຊອກນາຟອນ

Cthulhu: ຂະຕູຫຼູ

Dagon: ເດກອນ

Hastur: ຮາສ໌ ເຕ

Mi-Go: ມໂກ

Nyarlathotep: ຍາລາໂຕແຕບ

Shoggoth: ໂຊກອດ

Yig: ຍກ

Yog Sothoth: ຍອກຊໍ ຕອດ

About the Author

Bryan Thao Worra was born in 1973 in Vientiane, Laos during the Laotian Civil War. He came to the U.S. at six months old, adopted by a civilian pilot flying in Laos. In 2003, he reunited with his biological family after 30 years, during his first return to Laos.

As an award-winning writer, he has work appearing in numerous international anthologies, magazines and newspapers, including *Innsmouth Free Press, Kartika Review, Outsiders Within, Bamboo Among the Oaks, Tales of the Unanticipated, Astropoetica, Quarterly Literary Review Singapore, Whistling Shade, Journal of the Asian American Renaissance,* and *Asian American Press.*

In 2009, he became the first Laotian American to receive an NEA Fellowship In Literature. In 2012, he was a Cultural Olympian during the Summer Olympics in London, representing Laos.

He is the author of the books, *On the Other Side of the Eye, BARROW, Tanon Sai Jai,* and *Winter Ink.* Thao Worra has curated numerous readings and exhibits of Lao and Hmong American art, including *Legacies of War: Refugee Nation Twin Cities* (2010), *Emerging Voices* (2002), *The 5 Senses Show* (2002), *Lao'd and Clear* (2003), *Giant Lizard Theater* (2005), *Re:Generations* (2005), and *The Un-Named Series* (2007).

You can visit him online at: http://thaoworra.blogspot.com.

About the Artist

Vongduane Manivong was born in Vientiane, the capital city of Laos, and spent part of her childhood there. In the late 80s, she came to America with her parents when they fled the troubled country, finally settling in Dallas, Texas.

The Laotian diaspora in the wake
of the Vietnam War is a subtle-yet-poignant subtext running through much of her work. The war, which engulfed the entirety of what had once been known as Indochina, signified a torturous moment in history when tradition and modernity collided head-on. Her depictions of the daily lives of her people around the world form a body of work essential to understanding contemporary Laotian culture.

Her work encompasses a variety of artistic influences, from classical to pop, but it is the emotional core of the work that resonates most powerfully.

Vongduane's art has been exhibited in galleries across country, as well as at many national events, including the Symposium of Lao History at the University of California-Berkley, the National Youth Leadership Council's Urban Institute, and the Cultural Heritage Exhibition at the Laotian Community Center of Rhode Island.

These exhibitions have allowed her to bring wider attention to the diversity of the Laotian experience around the world.

You can visit her online at: http://www.vmpaintings.com.
.

About the Publisher

Innsmouth Free Press is a Canadian micro-publisher of Weird books based out of Vancouver, BC. In existence since 2009, it is responsible for the anthologies *Historical Lovecraft, Future Lovecraft* and *Fungi.*

Learn more about its titles at innsmouthfreepress.com

Acknowledgements

"Idle Fears," *Buddhist Poetry Review*, 2012.

"The Deep Ones," *Illumen,* 2007.

"Fragment of a Dream of Atlantean Yellows," "Dead End in December," *Innsmouth Free Press*, 2012.

"Songkran Niyomsane's Forensic Medicine Museum," "Ba," "Dream," "Democracia," "Temporary Passages," "The Tiger Penned At Kouangsi Falls," *On the Other Side of the Eye*, 2007.

"The Last War Poem," "The Spirit Catches You and You Get Body Slammed," *Bamboo Among the Oaks*, 2002.

"No Such Phi," *Lakeside Circus,* November, 2013.

"Kinnaly," *Tanon Sai Jai*, 2009.

"Stainless Steel Nak," *Lontar,* 2013.

"Dreamonstration," *North By Northside,* 2012.

"Destroy All Monsters!," "Song of the Kaiju," "The Moth," "The Big G Walking," "Kaiju Haiku," *G-Fan Magazine,* 2006.

"Projections through a Glass Eye," *Kartika Review,* 2011.

"Swallowing the Moon," *BARROW,* 2009.

"What Is The Southeast Asian American Poem of Tomorrow?" *Angry Asian Man*, 2012.